I0557904

DESSERTS AND DEATH

A PINK CUPCAKE MYSTERY BOOK 6

HARPER LIN

This is a work of fiction. Names, characters, organizations, places, events, and incidents are either products of the author's imagination or are used fictitiously.

DESSERTS AND DEATH

Copyright © 2018 by Harper Lin.

All rights reserved.

No part of this book may be reproduced, or stored in a retrieval system, or transmitted in any form or by any means, electronic, mechanical, photocopying, recording, or otherwise, without express written permission of the author.

ISBN-13: 978-1987859560

ISBN-10: 1987859561

www.harperlin.com

"I CAN'T BELIEVE I can't keep up with these receipts." Lila Bergman huffed, blowing a flaming-red curl of hair away from her face. "No disrespect, Amelia, but I never expected this little food truck to become so busy."

Amelia beamed and nodded as she pulled another batch of cinnamon-apple cupcakes out of the oven and set it on the counter behind the service window. The Pink Cupcake food truck had turned out to be a slice of heaven for her.

"Can you take a break from that and help me get the crumbles on the tops of these while I start the next batch?" she asked Lila. "I hate to admit that I thought the same thing when we first started."

Lila stood, grabbed the container of crumbles, and began to add the sugary topping to the steaming-hot cupcakes.

"Has John ever said good job or anything to you?"

Amelia's face wrinkled at the mention of her ex-husband.

"He still has issues with it. Can you believe that?" Amelia set the timer and planted one hand on her hip while she wiped her brow with the other. "To him, it's still just an offensive hot-pink truck that I bake out of. He has no idea how much money I'm putting into the business or how much I'm making, and even if he did, he'd find something wrong with it."

Lila shook her head.

"But thankfully, the wedding planning and honeymoon have occupied his mind enough that he's stayed out of my business for several glorious weeks."

"When is he due back?" Lila asked while setting the cinnamon-apple cupcakes on the rack for customers to see. "This batch of cupcakes smells just like apples off the tree. Did you know that? It makes the whole truck smell so good. I think these are my favorite when it comes to smells."

"He's back in another week." Amelia washed her hands in the sink and wiped some of the water on her face to cool off. Her cheeks were red from the ovens, which had been running hot since six in the morning. "It's been as much of a vacation for me without having him calling every couple of days to complain about one thing or another."

"Has he ever asked to see the books?" Lila asked.

"He's never come outright and asked, but I can tell it's driving him crazy to know. It's funny because I think *he* thinks I don't remember living with him for all those years." Amelia chuckled. "Attorneys don't come right out and ask anything. They hint around the topic and get you to say what they want without you realizing it."

"Sheesh. It's like being married to a Svengali."

"That's right." Amelia chuckled again. "So he makes comments like I probably don't have money to pay the property taxes, or he asks how much he'll have to kick in for the kids' year of school, hoping I'll complain I have no money. I know that's what he's hoping. He used to talk that way about opposing councils and clients he was representing. He's forgotten I learned his tactics a long time ago. Frankly, my life now is none of his business."

"Well, I think he'd be kicking himself if he saw those receipts. You are really turning a profit."

"Yeah, well, I don't have the tuition for Yale and Harvard for the kids socked away yet, so to me it's still a long row to hoe."

"How are the kids handling their new, ahem, stepmom?"

Amelia laughed outright as she watched Lila's face contort as if she'd just eaten a lemon.

"You know the kids. They aren't babies anymore, and they aren't stupid. If Jennifer is nice to them, they will be nice back. I've told them that she's their father's wife now."

"And they're good with that?" Lila prodded. "They know there is no chance of Mom and Dad getting back together?"

"I think they knew that a long time ago, Lila. Now I just want them to be decent stepchildren. It would break my heart if I ever found out that Jennifer was saying they were obnoxious or disrespectful or nasty. Of course, the urge might be there. Heck, I feel like telling the princess to take a long walk off a short pier constantly. But I've talked with the kids, and they want smooth sailing as much as I do. As much as John does, too."

"You're lucky. Not all families have enough common sense to make things easy on themselves. I have to say I am glad that Jacob and I never had children for this specific reason. The babies are so innocent."

"That they are. Have you heard anything from Jacob lately?"

"Oh, yes," Lila gushed. "He made a lovely deposit in my bank account this very month. Looks like the ponies paid off extra dividends."

"He was a gambler?"

"Yes. He was actually quite good at it. But when you don't have to worry about losing ten thousand dollars at the track, it sort of takes the edge off."

"What?" Amelia barked. "He lost ten thousand dollars at the horse track? Are you kidding me?"

Lila laughed and waved her hand in front of her face as she usually did when something was no big deal to her.

"I don't think he ever lost that much. He's lost a few times, but like I said, he had a real talent. When he won big, he usually came home with a bottle of champagne. That's how I'd know. Of course, in retrospect, he usually left with a bottle, too. I should have known where he was going." She laughed. "Oh, isn't youth wasted on the young? If I knew then what I know now, I would have never worried about Jacob. "

"That it is." Amelia stretched her back and went to the service window. Then she noticed the top of someone's head. Amelia saw a daddy, and as she looked to where the giggles were coming from, she saw he was accompanied by twin boys. The little guys couldn't have been more than five or six years old.

"Can I get two of your PB and J cupcakes, please?" the man asked while pulling out his money.

"Is it boys' day out?" Amelia asked cheerfully.

"Yeah. It's Mommy's birthday, so she gets to sleep in and then go do some shopping alone." The man chuckled.

"Well, in that case, PB and Js are on us." She handed the man two huge peanut butter and jelly cupcakes in a hot-pink paper boat with an extra couple of napkins.

"That's really kind of you."

"Don't mention it."

"Hey, you wouldn't happen to have a healthy cupcake back there? You know, something that used soy milk or applesauce or something." The man wrinkled his nose. "She's trying to lose weight. Not that she needs to, but it would be a nice surprise."

"Gosh, you know, we don't, but that is a really good idea." Amelia looked at Lila, who winked her approval.

"Well, I'm sure we'll be back," the man replied. "Thanks again." He handed the cupcakes to his sons, and both Amelia and Lila watched him walk both of them to a picnic table to eat.

"How sweet." Lila folded her arms over her chest. "And what a good idea."

"Right?" Amelia exclaimed, her eyes wide with excitement. "Different ingredients, same sweetness. I love it!"

"Can you do it?" Lila's voice hinted at more of a challenge than a question. She knew if anyone could make a healthy cupcake taste good, it would be Amelia.

"*We* can do it. Totally. We can do it." Amelia grabbed a small notebook from her purse and began to scribble down ideas. "I think keeping it simple at first will be our best bet, and let's stay away from carrot or zucchini because those are done to death."

"Yes. I agree. How about a green tea flavor?" Lila suggested. "I just had some green tea ice cream when I went out for Chinese food yesterday, and it was very good."

"That sounds perfect."

"What happened to you?" Lila cried out suddenly.

Amelia looked up to see Lila looking past her out the service window. She turned to look and gasped.

"Goodness! Dan!"

CHAPTER TWO

DETECTIVE DAN WALISHOVSKI stood looking up at Amelia with a bandage on his forehead and his arm in a sling.

Amelia dashed out of the back door of the truck and rushed to Dan's side. It could be hard dating a detective, as it wasn't Mayberry they lived in, where everyone knew everyone and the worst the police had to deal with was the town drunk taking up space in one of the two holding cells that were normally used for their weekly poker game. This was Gary, Oregon, where murders and crime were surprisingly common.

"What happened to you?" Amelia exclaimed.

"Is this why you couldn't come by last night? Why didn't you tell me? Does it hurt? What happened?"

"If you'll slow down and just take a breath, I'll explain everything," Dan said. His eyes were a bright blue. As Amelia looked up into them, she saw the familiar twinkle that assured her he had a story to tell.

"Uh-oh." Amelia stood back. "This looks like it's going to be quite a tale. Want to come up and sit?"

"Don't mind if I do. Lila, you got any coffee up there?"

"For you, Detective, I sure do."

Amelia climbed back up into the truck and pulled a stool out for Dan to sit by the door, where a cool breeze was some relief from the heat of the ovens.

"Smells good in here," Dan observed as he took a paper cup full of coffee from Lila. "What are you two ladies cooking up in here?"

"Cinnamon-apple crumbles. Here, eat one. Lila came up with a great idea for a new healthier version of a cupcake for our health-conscious friends."

"Oh, I'll be diving into those." Dan patted his

stomach. "But until then..." He happily accepted the cupcake, taking a bite and chewing slowly.

"Okay, I appreciate your enjoying the cupcake, but are you going to tell me what happened, or do I have to guess?" Amelia urged.

"Let me guess," Lila interrupted. "There was a fight between a couple of fourth graders at the school, and you got caught breaking it up."

"No. No. Not fourth graders. A couple of rowdy seniors at the center over a bingo dispute." Amelia chuckled.

"Two middle-aged women were fighting over the latest Disney-themed bed set, and you were on the losing team."

"You ladies are hilarious," Dan said as he took a sip of coffee. "But the truth isn't that far off. You just aren't going to believe this."

The Gary Police Department, like every other police department in the country, had come to recognize certain addresses, phone numbers, and individuals when those calls came through the dispatcher. Some were like clockwork. Every Friday night around one o'clock in the morning, there was a call from Pat's Pub that there were a couple of guys fighting in the parking lot. A couple times a month, the neighbors around 4201 Christine Way called to report the residents were fighting again. The casino on the outskirts of town had half a dozen calls a week to report drunk-and-disorderly conduct.

But a call from Bud Fetzer was different. Dan explained to Amelia and Lila that Bud was a very interesting fellow.

"I doubt he's thirty years old," Dan reported. "He lives alone, has no record, has some kind of computer gig that he does out of his house. UFO conspiracies. JFK cover-up. Some nonsense about the earth being hollow."

"That's his job? UFOs?" Lila inquired.

"Yup. He's got quite a following, from what I hear. But to hear him tell it, he's public enemy number one for what he calls anti-truth individuals. That was what he was calling about. As usual."

Dan went on to tell Amelia and Lila that once every two or three months, they'd get a call to stop by the Fetzer place. It was a simple ranch house on a pristine piece of land that was left to Bud by his late parents. Mr. and Mrs. Fetzer had invested wisely over the years. They only had one son. So when they passed on, they had made sure their pride and joy was taken care of.

"What?" Amelia stifled a laugh. "Did *he* do this to you?"

"Not quite." Dan rolled his eyes.

Dan went on to explain the call that he received from dispatch. A squad car had already shown up at the Fetzer property in response to Bud's call saying there was a suspicious truck with two suspicious individuals lurking around his property.

"The uniforms said they checked everything out, and there were tire tracks and footprints but nothing that would lead them to believe that it was anything more than just a truck that stopped on the side of the road." Dan took another sip from his coffee. "But Bud wasn't satisfied with that. He needed me out there. Requested me by name. Said he and I had an understanding."

Amelia watched Dan roll his eyes and started to giggle.

"Did you?"

"Not quite. Bud had come to the station a couple times, complaining about people on his property and hearing low-frequency radio sounds in his house. I got the assignment to check out his property and found absolutely nothing of substance. But I talked with Bud, and for all intents and purposes, he was a real nice guy," Dan admitted while gently tapping the bandage on his forehead. "When I knocked on his door and announced who I was, the camera he installed at his front door came loose just as I was looking up into it. That's what caused this."

"What happened to your arm?" Amelia asked, fretting.

"After getting hit on the head, I lost my balance and fell off his porch, dislocating my shoulder and spraining my wrist."

Lila didn't stifle her laughter.

"Well, did you find anything at his house that little green men were planning an attack or something?" Amelia asked playfully.

"No," he replied sourly. "If that were the case, at least I would have gotten hurt for a reason. Now I gotta hear the guys at the station ribbing me about being abducted and possibly probed."

Amelia and Lila couldn't help but burst out laughing.

"We don't mean to laugh at you," Amelia said between bursts of giggles.

"She doesn't. I do," Lila teased as she refilled Dan's coffee.

"You're all about that tough love, aren't you, Lila?" Dan snickered back.

"I think you should head on over to my house," Amelia suggested. "I've got beef stew in the crockpot already cooking. Plus, Lila came up with a genius new idea for a cupcake, and I'll need tasters. What do you say?"

"I say that sounds pretty good." Dan gave Amelia a cool grin. "I've got to go to the station and wrap up some paperwork. I'll meet you at your place after you close up shop."

"That sounds fine."

By the time Amelia closed up the Pink Cupcake and drove home, she was exhausted. The idea of hiring on additional help was looking better and better all the time. She was happy to see Dan's sedan parked in front of the house. He was just getting out of the car.

"Have you been waiting long?" Amelia asked as she parked her business in her driveway.

"Nope. Just got here a second ago. Turns out that Bud Fetzer wanted to speak with me at the station."

"Really? I'm intrigued."

"He swears there are people watching his house."

Amelia bit her lower lip.

"Do you think there is any truth to what he's saying?"

Dan shrugged, wincing as he rubbed his arm.

"I don't know. But to tell you the truth, tonight I don't want to talk about work or Bud or conspiracies. I'd give all the tea in China just to hear Meg's latest school gossip or Adam's most recent computer project."

"Have you been drinking?" Amelia teased. "That's hardcore."

"No. But I think I might start."

Once they were in the house, Dan got his wish. Amelia drank a bottle of beer with him.

"Katherine told me that she has an aunt that is totally convinced that there are lizard people in the government," Meg piped up over her bowl of stew. "She says they are part of the Illuminati."

"I don't know about lizards. Snakes would be more like it," Amelia said to Dan as she filled his bowl with stew.

"The Illuminati. That's crazy." Adam sniggered.

"She also said that her aunt saw a UFO. Just a tiny little weird white thing in the sky that changed direction super fast. I don't know if it's true. I never met this aunt."

"You never will. They only allow family to visit people in the booby-hatch," Adam continued.

"No one asked you, Adam," Meg snapped.

"Adam, do we say booby-hatch? Really?" Amelia pursed her lips at her son. "That's not very nice."

"Sorry, Mom." Adam chuckled.

"I heard people say that Kennedy wasn't assassinated by Lee Harvey Oswald and that it was a CIA cover-up," Meg added before taking a mouthful of bread she had dunked in her stew.

Dan looked across the table at Amelia, who was grinning with amusement.

"I'm just glad she knows who Kennedy and Lee Harvey Oswald were," she said before finally sitting down and starting to eat.

Meg carried on her conversation about UFOs and aliens while Adam interrupted, adding the fact that NASA and the SETI projects relied on computers to search for signals of intelligence in space.

Amelia and Dan sat quietly listening as the kids argued and joked and dominated the conversation at the table, giving the grown-ups a chance to unwind.

Finally, after deciding that aliens do exist but

would never come near Adam because he's too big of a nerd and that Meg would bore them to death, triggering an intergalactic war, the kids retreated to their rooms to start their homework.

"Maybe coming here wasn't the best idea," Amelia joked. "It's not always a fortress of silence."

"I've come to enjoy it. It's my favorite part of the day, to tell you the truth."

"You're an easy man to please, Detective." Amelia took a deep breath and patted her full stomach. "Are you interested in keeping me company while I work on this new recipe?"

"Tell me it requires tons of butter and cream and sugar."

"Actually, I'm thinking of a green tea cupcake."

Dan wrinkled his nose.

"You may as well have said a broccoli and Brussels sprout cupcake."

"Come on. You've had green tea ice cream?"

"Where in the world would I ever eat that?" Dan stood up and helped Amelia reach into a top cabinet for a bag of flour.

"At a Chinese restaurant," Amelia answered, taking the bag and bumping Dan with her hip. "I'm making it with applesauce instead of sugar, and I'll be using almond milk instead of the hard stuff. And instead of frosting, I was thinking a light dusting of confectioners' sugar."

"That sounds real pretty. But I'll believe it when I taste it." Dan had been in Amelia's kitchen more than once when she was baking and had learned where she kept most of her supplies. As she grabbed the jars of applesauce and a small bottle of vanilla extract, he got her mixing bowls, measuring cups and spoons, and electric blender.

As she started to dabble with the basic ingredients, slowly measuring them, she couldn't help but ask about Bud.

"He lives in a nice part of town," Amelia stated as she sifted the flour. "It's a shame that is what occupies his time."

"The guy is really no trouble. Just once every month or two he gets a bee in his bonnet. His nearest neighbor is Luann Jameson. You've heard of her, right?"

"Heard of her? Who hasn't?" Amelia's eyes widened at the mention of the woman. "Her real estate business is blasted all over every park bench and billboard across town."

"Yeah, she's got to love having that Fort Knox bunker on the adjoining property." Dan harrumphed.

"Why would you say that?"

"You've obviously never seen the Jameson property."

Amelia shook her head.

"Her late husband left her quite a bit of scratch. Plus, the real estate in Gary has always been a cash cow for those who know how to work it. From what I gather, she does. The place is professionally maintained. Flowers, shrub sculptures, koi ponds, aesthetically lit at nighttime. It is quite a sight."

"Well, Luann is quite a sight, too."

The billboard images of Luann Jameson didn't do her justice even though they were the most flawless glamour shots ever taken. With blond hair down her back and a 36DD chest in front, also compliments of her late husband, Luann was someone everyone knew about. But unless you were looking into buying one of her properties in Sarkis Estates, she had very little use for you.

"Her daughter looks just like her," Dan added.

"I never see her," Amelia said. "She's been kept under wraps for years."

"Yeah. She's real protective of her. We had a unit go out to the property because someone had vandalized their mailbox along with half a dozen others on the same stretch of road. Her daughter,

Colleen, was telling the officer about finding the mailbox in pieces. Just a normal girl giving the facts, and Luann pulled in the driveway, yelling like a banshee for the girl to go inside."

"Yikes."

Dan leaned on the counter.

"The uniformed officer said that Luann told him to get any ideas about dating her daughter out of his head."

"Really?"

"Yup. Officer Harvey was engaged to a real sweet girl. Patricia, I think her name was," Dan continued. "Didn't matter to Luann. She was convinced that everyone was out to get her daughter. 'No daughter of mine is going to date a civil servant.'"

"She really said that?"

Dan nodded and gave a slight eye roll.

"How old is Colleen now?"

"She's got to be in her early twenties, and she still lives with Luann."

"Who does she want her daughter to marry?"

"Anyone with a seven-figure bank account is my guess."

Amelia measured out the applesauce in the correct proportions to take the place of the sugar and tasted the batter before deciding it needed one more scoop.

"Maybe I'm a bad mother," Amelia admitted. "I've never talked about that kind of stuff with Meg. I mean, she's still just a baby, but I know soon enough boys are going to become important. I just want her to be happy."

"Most mothers think the way you do."

"Is John back from his honeymoon yet?" Dan asked, letting her know it was okay to talk about it.

"Does it show on my face that much?"

"No. I've just learned how to read you a little bit." Dan took a step closer to her.

"He gets back next week," Amelia admitted. "I had that big bank account, too. It went with John when he left. Now it's Jennifer's."

"Does that bother you?"

"It does and it doesn't. He pays his alimony, and that is enough to cover expenses for school and little else. I was just telling Lila today he is desperate to know about the books on the Pink Cupcake, but I'd rather cut off my own arm than tell him the truth. I'm nowhere near retirement, but Christmas ought to be a good one this year. We should be able to get the big goose hanging in the butcher shop before Mr. Scrooge does." She winked playfully.

Dan slipped his arms around Amelia's waist.

"I don't have a fortune to offer you, Amelia. I wish I did."

"That isn't what I'm saying at all, Dan. You know that." Amelia leaned against him. "I'm just wondering if Luann is really all bad for encouraging her daughter to find someone who can provide for her in that way."

"How would you feel about a woman dating Adam for his money? Would you tell him that a girl like that would be a wise endeavor?"

"You got me there. No. I wouldn't."

"That kind of puts things in perspective, doesn't it?"

"Yeah."

"So what other kinds of poison are you adding to these health muffins?" Dan asked, kissing Amelia on the top of the head.

"You're going to love these." She stepped back to her mixing bowl and continued to stir the batter. "I don't have a fortune to offer you, either, Dan. But you'll get all the cupcakes you can swallow for as long as you like."

"I'll take it."

CHAPTER THREE

"SO THE MINUTE John is back from his honeymoon, he's calling you to renegotiate the alimony?" Lila nearly choked the words out. "I don't think I need to spell out whose idea that was."

"Right?" Amelia dumped a cup of flour in a bowl so hard it mushroom-clouded up into her face. "I told him to have his lawyer contact my lawyer and that I was not even going to entertain the idea. You know what it is? He is so desperate to know what kind of money the Pink Cupcake is making, and this is the only way to find out."

"You want me to cook up a special batch of books for you? I can do it," Lila said, her face as serious as a tombstone.

"What? No. It's not worth going to jail for."

"What jail? Who is going to look into the validity of the financial records of a small time baker-slash-divorcee with a food truck?"

"You can't be serious." Amelia chuckled.

"I did it for Jacob."

Amelia stared at her friend.

"Don't look so shocked. That's another reason he sends such a sizable check every month. Hush money." She winked.

"Lila." Amelia felt the need to whisper. "Cooking the books is a felony."

"If you get caught, yes, that is what I think it is." She shrugged. "But it's not like I did it all the time. Some years were harder than others. Jacob asked for a little help, and so I did what I could. I'm good with numbers."

"That you are." Amelia grinned. "And I appreciate your risking your freedom to help me out."

"What are friends for?"

"Well, usually they are to talk you out of making bad decisions, but in this case I see it's with a giving heart you are offering to help."

The ladies continued to talk, when a female voice interrupted their conversation.

"Excuse me, do you have any of those double-chocolate raspberry cupcakes left?" Amelia turned and looked straight into the blue eyes of Colleen Jameson.

"We've got a fresh batch just coming out of the oven. Can you give me about five minutes?" Amelia grinned.

"That's fine," the young lady chirped. Her demeanor seemed to be the complete opposite of her mother, who Amelia had heard was as demanding with her mortgage negotiations as she was buying tomatoes at a vegetable stand.

After ringing up Colleen's sale, Amelia watched her walk away and realized how right Dan was. She looked just like her mother with an unstoppable hourglass figure, blond hair, and blue eyes. The thing that wasn't like her mother was the man Colleen was holding hands with.

"Lila," Amelia whispered, tossing her head to get her to come to the service window. "Who is that man? I've seen him before."

"That's Greg Scottson."

"I thought so. He's worked on my car a couple times not that long ago." Amelia bit her lower lip. "He's over there at the Gary Service Center. Does he own that place?"

"Ha!" Lila laughed. "No. Nelson Leman owns that place. He's been the main mechanic in town for years. That's his place. He's a nice fellow but a little pushy, if you know what I mean." Lila adjusted the collar of her blouse.

"Yes. I knew that. I've had Nelson work on my car a few times, too. Now that I think about it, I think every mechanic over there has seen under my hood. Maybe it's time I get a new car. Wait. Did Nelson make a pass at you?"

"No. He's after my Cadillac."

Amelia shook her head.

"That's funny we see her today. Dan and I were talking about her just last week, and Dan told me her mother…"

"Her mother is an interesting woman," Lila offered. "I've only seen her a handful of times. From what I hear, she's a real workaholic. You'd have to be to pay the property taxes on that chunk of land she owns. Or should I say inherited. Anyway, the last time I saw her at the hair salon, she was getting that mane of hers trimmed, and she just gushed over the woman trimming her hair as if she were creating a Rembrandt."

"Is that weird?"

"Well, it was just a little over-the-top. But what do I know? I'm as over-the-top as they come, so I shouldn't be throwing stones."

"Dan told me she was real protective of her daughter."

"Now that is an understatement. I've seen Colleen out but never without Luann at most five paces behind her. But you know how mothers can be. Colleen's not just her only daughter, but her only child."

"So isn't it weird that her daughter is with Greg? Alone?"

"Yes. It's weird. Definitely." Lila stood on her tiptoes to get a better look at the couple. "But maybe Greg jumped through all the right hoops? Or maybe Luann decided it was time to give her daughter some space. It's anyone's guess."

Amelia finished the cupcakes then popped them carefully into the pink paper boats with a couple napkins. She strolled out to the picnic table where the couple was sitting across from each other, holding hands.

"Here you go, guys. Sorry for the wait."

"I'd wait a lot longer than that for your cupcakes. My mom brings them home all the time," Colleen bubbled.

"Really?" Amelia knew what her mother looked like and was sure she had never once seen her at the Pink Cupcake. She might have had her assistant come get them for her.

"I just love them. These are my favorite. I'll have to do an extra three-story climb on the Stairmaster, but it's so worth it."

"I am so glad you like them."

"Do you cater?"

"As a matter of fact, we do. Any occasion, and we can custom-design your cupcakes to fit your theme."

Colleen looked at Greg and pulled her shoulders up to her ears and grinned giddily. He raised his eyebrows but said nothing.

At the same time, Amelia pulled a hot-pink business card from her pocket.

"If you've got an event coming up, please give me a call."

"We will. It might be my mom calling. Her name is Luann Jameson."

At the mention of Luann's name, Greg leaned back as if the words might bite him. He pinched the skin right above his nose.

"What?" Colleen asked innocently.

Greg shook his head but still said nothing.

"I've seen your mom's picture around town. I know who she is." Amelia smiled. "Just tell her I'll be happy to answer any questions."

"I will." It seemed that Colleen was only like her mother in the looks department. She was friendly and almost hysterically chipper.

Amelia thanked Colleen, wished her a good day, and came back to the truck, shrugging to Lila.

"Nothing weird there?"

That afternoon, Amelia had a chance to tell Dan when he called about her coincidental encounter with the mysterious Colleen Jameson.

"And you saw her with who?" Amelia could hear the surprise in Dan's voice.

"With Greg Scottson."

"No. That can't be."

"I'm telling you. Ask Lila if you don't believe me."

"Are you sure it wasn't some guy who looked like Greg?"

"I'm sure. They came and bought cupcakes from us. Well, Colleen paid, but they were right at the service window and then took a seat at the picnic table, and I had a pleasant chat with her for several minutes. Why is this so hard to believe?"

Dan cleared his throat.

"For one, Greg Scottson has a record."

"Really?"

"Yeah, and we're not talking petty theft either." Dan went on, "About six years ago, he was arrested for lewd behavior with a minor. He said the fifteen-year-old girl in his car said she was eighteen. He was twenty-two at the time."

Amelia couldn't help but immediately think of Meg. She was only fourteen herself and so pretty and bubbly. The thought of her being in the same room as someone who thought like that made her skin crawl.

"The evidence seemed to jibe with what he said, but due to the nature of the crime and the judge presiding, there was no way Greg was going to get off without something. He got three years' probation. In that time, he was arrested for public intoxication a couple of times and possession of a misdemeanor amount of marijuana on his person."

"I'm sorry," Amelia interrupted. "But didn't you tell me that Colleen's mother held some pretty tight reins when it came to her precious daughter and who she was allowed to date?"

"I did. Why do you think I'm so shocked?"

"Well, they were holding hands when I saw them. Gazing into each other's eyes like two people I know," she teased.

"How in the world did those two even meet?"

"Come on, Detective. You mean to tell me you can't figure that out?" Dan could see Amelia's smirk over the phone, and it made him grin. "Obviously, her mother took her Lexus in to Nelson's for some work. That might even require a couple trips there. Plenty of time for him to get to know Colleen."

"You might be right. Very good, Miss Harley."

Amelia smiled at the smile in Dan's voice. "I might have to pop by and have a couple words with Nelson and see if this is what we think it is."

"Well, Greg isn't lacking in the looks area. You know how some women fall for a bad-boy reputation and a handsome face. Look at me."

Amelia laughed. "I'll probably be left in ruin before all is said and done."

It was true that whatever Greg was lacking in smarts he made up for in looks. He had wild black naturally wavy hair that reminded Amelia of Kurt Russell in his younger days. His shoulders were broad, and there didn't seem to be any kind of paunch or gut hanging over his belt.

"Right." Dan scoffed. "Even with his criminal

history, he's never had a problem with the ladies. I think that's part of the reason Nelson keeps him at the garage because of all the girls that come looking for him."

"And here I thought Nelson was just a harmless old grease-monkey, and it turns out he has a deviant side."

"I wouldn't call Nelson deviant. He just has a pulse. You can't blame a man for looking at what someone has put on display."

"I suppose." Amelia had never been much of an exhibitionist, and she hoped her conservative ways had rubbed off on Meg. So far, she hadn't had any problems.

"But then there are those guys who like a little more substance to their women. A good head on their shoulders. Common sense. A sense of humor. That's what's attractive."

"You really think so?"

"Yes, Miss Harley, and I don't just think so. I know so."

"Well, I have to agree with Lila that youth is wasted on the young."

"That sounds like a Lila-ism. I couldn't agree more." Amelia could hear someone talking to Dan in the background. It was obvious he was being called back to work.

"Honey, I have to go."

Amelia got goose bumps hearing Dan call her honey. It was such a little thing, but she knew it wasn't a term a guy like him tossed around. She felt as if he'd just given her a bouquet of sunflowers.

"Okay, come by later if you like."

"I'll try, but I might have to take a rain check. I'll call you."

When Amelia hung up, she thought that maybe she should have a talk with Meg about the way things worked in the world. Maybe the girl already knew. The things teenagers bantered around to each other were about ten percent fact and ninety percent fiction, but it would be worth talking to her about. The last thing she wanted was for her to get carried away over the first guy who told her she was pretty.

"I should talk to Adam, too. What's good for the goose, and all that mumbo-jumbo." That talk made her stomach tie up in knots. It wasn't that she feared the worst for her son. At seventeen, he was a smart kid, and he did march to the beat of his own drum. But other than Amy down the street, Amelia didn't know if he had an interest in any other girls or if he knew how important it was to be a gentleman.

Taking a deep breath, she grabbed the bottle of water she had been nursing while she took a ten-minute break outside the truck. With one giant swig, she went back into the hot box and began a batch of vanilla cherry cupcakes.

CHAPTER FOUR

"I'M SO glad you could come by." Amelia took Lila's jacket as she stepped inside the house. "I'm sorry it had to be on the rainiest day of the season."

"When there is a cupcake crisis, you can bet that I'll come running." Lila handed Amelia her wet coat and propped her umbrella in the corner. "What's happening?"

"These green tea cupcakes." Amelia sighed. "They are missing something, and I don't want to throw in the towel just yet. I think if I have a second set of taste buds, maybe together we can figure out what's missing."

"How would you describe what they taste like?" Lila followed Amelia into the kitchen.

"I'd say sort of cardboard-y."

They laughed.

"It just has no flavor. It isn't that it tastes bad. It doesn't taste like anything. I've added vanilla extract and almond extract, but there is something in the matcha that is swallowing up all the competing flavors. It's like a culinary black hole."

"Sounds like we need something with a little more kick."

Amelia handed her a green cupcake and waited for the verdict. "Gross, right?"

"Not totally. But bland to be sure." The ladies discussed all the ingredients, and finally, Lila made a bold suggestion.

"What if we add a little honey to the mix?"

Amelia stared into her pantry. She reached in and pulled out a little plastic bear filled with honey. Then she gasped.

"What about a little of this, too?" It was coconut extract.

Lila's eyes popped.

"That's worth a try." She took a seat at the table while Amelia began whipping together the ingredients. She had made several attempts before calling Lila, so the first half of the recipe was almost totally committed to memory. She carefully measured off a dab of honey and the drops of extract before tasting the batter.

"Better?" Lila asked before sticking her own finger in the batter.

"I think this might work." Amelia clapped giddily. "If it does, we are going to have to charge a little more because this coconut extract is a lot more expensive than vanilla."

"If we market it as a fancy-pants healthy alternative, people will pay a little more. That would be the last thing I'd worry about." Lila grabbed the newspaper that was on the counter. "Speaking of worry. Where is your brood?"

"Meg is at Katherine's house. Adam is at Amy's house."

"A nice quiet afternoon for Mama, and there's no wine?"

"How about a Baileys and coffee?" Amelia suggested.

"Now you're talking." Lila unfolded the paper and started perusing the headlines. "I don't know what I'm looking at this for. There isn't any good news or interesting factoids. Even the weather is negative."

"Yeah, but I get the sale papers in there, and sometimes I read the obituaries."

"Whoa!" Lila barked. "Now this is news!"

"What is it?"

"Colleen Marie Jameson is engaged to Gregory Timber Scottson…"

"Timber?"

Lila shrugged as she continued reading.

"The nuptials are scheduled for one month from today."

Both ladies looked at each other.

"Dare I say it?" Lila smirked.

"Let me save you the trouble. Shotgun?"

"That's all I can think of. Well, it certainly isn't the worst thing to happen to a person. But I'd have given just about anything to have been a fly on the wall during that conversation with the new mother-in-law."

Amelia shook her head as she set the timer for fifteen minutes.

"You know, it's easy to pass judgment, but we don't know the story. Perhaps the kids really are in love. Sure, she is as green as a valley in springtime, but that doesn't mean it isn't real."

"I find it interesting you say that." Lila folded her arms over her chest and studied Amelia.

"Don't you have hope for true love?" Amelia asked. "A fairytale ending?"

Lila smiled and finally nodded. "I remember my wedding."

"I'll bet it was beautiful." Amelia poured them each a steaming cup of coffee and added a shot of Baileys into each one.

"It was nice. I had a beautiful dress. My brides-maids were decent enough gals that there wasn't any infighting or cattiness. But I remember people always saying to me, 'Don't worry when something goes wrong.' Who tells a bride-to-be that?"

Amelia leaned in.

"I'd mention I was getting married, and some old biddy would tell me how her cake was dropped on the floor or the hall didn't have enough seats or her dress didn't fit right. If something can go wrong, it will. So many women said that."

"That happened to me, too." Amelia shrugged. "Little did I know that it wasn't the wedding day. It was the two decades later that caused all the problems."

"I was convinced that if the groom showed up, the wedding day would be a success. It proved to be right. There might have been a couple of hitches here or there, but I don't remember them. I just remember walking down that aisle and seeing Jacob. He looked so handsome. It didn't matter to me what else happened that day. As long as the priest got through the words 'I now pronounce you man and wife,' I was a happy bride."

"Yeah, I have to admit that John looked quite handsome, too. Back then, he smiled when he saw me. Not like now. His face is so sour it's like he's got a lemon wedge stuck in his cheek."

"I doubt that is all his doing." Lila nodded knowingly. "He must have said a few things about you to Jennifer that make her feel a little insecure. Think about it. You're going to be the mother of his children forever. You're always going to be there, whether she takes his last name or not."

"Well, she did, and it's over and done with. Now Colleen and Greg are headed down that path, and who knows. Maybe it will really be forever."

"Maybe," Lila grumbled, not even trying to hide her doubt. "I'll happily admit I was wrong, but I doubt I will be."

Once the ladies finished their cups of Baileys and coffee, the cupcakes were finished. They each took one and took a bite.

"It tastes like a non-alcoholic piña colada," Lila boasted.

"It does. This is a very smooth flavor. Light. It

tastes healthier." Amelia smiled. "Should we try a couple out tomorrow?"

"What are you thinking will frost these?" Lila said, taking another bite.

"Powdered sugar."

"Perfect."

As it turned out, there wasn't a huge demand for a healthier cupcake. By five o'clock, quitting time, Amelia had only made one dozen green tea cupcakes, and there was still one left that didn't have a home.

"I'm thinking maybe this would be something to promote during special times of the year. Like right after New Year's when people are feeling guilty because they chowed down all holiday season?" Amelia suggested.

"That is a great idea. I'll bet you'll clean up with that gimmick."

CHAPTER FIVE

ABOUT TWO MONTHS passed since she first tried the green tea cupcakes.

It wasn't often that Amelia's creations weren't a smashing success. This made her worry that there might be something wrong. A bad omen. But she didn't say anything to Lila or Dan or the kids.

It was something she needed to get through on her own. What she didn't want to admit to herself was that she was getting a little burnt out. She loved baking. She loved her truck. She certainly loved how she was getting her loans paid off. But there was a wall on the inside of her mind that she was sure was closing in a millimeter at a time.

"Maybe you need to exercise more," she'd

mumble at five in the morning as she drowsily came to work. "Or dare you take a vacation? Where on earth would you go? You can't leave the kids, and they can't miss school. Even if Lila offered to watch them, where is there to go that would be of any interest?"

She didn't have any answers to this, either, so it stayed deep inside her gut. A few weeks went by, and she realized she was sleeping later and rushing around in the morning, looking for her keys, her wallet, or the deposit bag.

By the time she pulled into her spot on Food Truck Alley, she was already exhausted.

"I need to hire someone," she said out loud. "I'll get Lila to write up a job description. Just so I can have an afternoon or morning shift to get some rest. That ought to do it. It's got to be just exhaustion."

For a minute, Amelia thought of Lila. She had had breast cancer, but it was gone now along with both her breasts. What were the warning signs? Was she tired a lot? Should Amelia get herself checked out?

"You are jumping to conclusions." She put the coffee on. "Go get a check-up if you're so worried." That idea scared her even more. "I don't know if I can afford a check-up right now. But that just sounds like a lame excuse to me. Yes, it does."

She sipped the hot coffee and switched on the ovens.

Today was going to be vanilla cherry cupcakes paired with lemon cupcakes. The frostings were almost identical and could be shared without jeopardizing the taste.

"It's rare to see you staring out into space." Dan's voice made Amelia jump and clutch her heart.

"What are you doing here so early?" She gasped before getting up to give him a peck on the cheek.

"Up so early? You mean up so late. I haven't even gone to bed yet."

"Busy night?"

"You have no idea."

Amelia went and poured Dan a cup of coffee.

"Have a seat while the truck is still cool on the inside." She dragged a stool from the corner for him to sit on. "So what kept you so busy?"

"Maybe you should be the one who takes a seat."

"Why?"

"I just came from Luann Jameson's house. Her

new son-in-law died yesterday evening around four o'clock."

"What?" Suddenly, Amelia's heart started racing.

"He was up on her roof, fixing some shingles. Slipped and fell from the top of that huge house and landed on the only piece of driveway exposed beneath the roof."

"That's terrible. Poor Colleen. She must be devastated."

"She didn't say too much. I think she is still in shock." Dan rubbed his face.

"Are they having a funeral and a wake? I don't know. I have a weird feeling maybe I should go." Amelia thought out loud. "No. I didn't know them all that well. Still, how sad."

"Yeah, well, like I thought would happen. According to Luann, Greg had been smoking pot and decided he was going to prove he was good at something. Climbed up on the roof and slid right off."

Amelia shook her head.

"That's not even the worst of it. Colleen is pregnant."

"Oh no." Amelia gasped, putting her hand to her chest.

"Oh yes. They didn't waste any time." Dan shook his head. "My head is throbbing. I gotta go. I'll call you tonight after I sleep the entire day."

"Of course. Would you like me to bring you something to eat?"

"Nope. Got a can of tomato soup with my name on it. I'll be fine."

Amelia continued getting the ovens preheated and starting on the day's recipes. But her mind kept drifting to that day she spoke with Colleen. She mentioned her mother, and Greg winced. It was the look of a man who didn't get along with his girl-friend's mother.

Amelia might have been a couple decades older than them, but she wasn't so old she didn't remember how a suitor acted around her parents when it was obvious they didn't like him. One-word answers to questions. Arms folded all the time. Plus an almost violent physical reaction when she would mention her parents. Not much had changed over the years.

"I hate to be the wet blanket at such a delicate time," Lila said after Amelia told her the news. "But if the guy was smoking weed and then went up on the roof, he obviously wasn't that bright. Maybe it was a blessing this happened."

"Lila, how can you say that?" Amelia smiled because she had been thinking the same thing but didn't have the guts to say it. Not so bluntly, anyway.

"I'm not saying I'm glad it happened. I'm just saying…"

Amelia was about to reply when her cell phone went off. It was a number she'd never seen before.

"The Pink Cupcake. Amelia speaking."

"Amelia Harley?"

"This is she."

"Miss Harley, this is Luann Jameson. My daughter picked up your business card some time back and said you catered."

"Yes, Miss Jameson. That's true. What can I do for you?"

Amelia stared at Lila, whose eyes bugged out of her head as her jaw dropped.

"I'm having an intimate affair for about one hundred people, and I was hoping you could accommodate. My daughter says the double-choco-late raspberry cupcakes are amazing. I have to take her word for it. I don't eat refined sugar of any kind."

Amelia pulled a pen from her purse and began

to scribble down what Luann was saying on the back of a receipt while she shrugged at Lila.

"One hundred double-chocolate raspberry cupcakes. Sure. When do you need them, and where should they be delivered?"

"I'll need them delivered to my house at 667 Lahon Road. It's the house with the pillars." She sounded bored. "Tomorrow around four o'clock in the afternoon."

"Yes, ma'am." Amelia agreed and took a credit card number before hanging up the phone with a "Thank you, Mrs. Jameson. See you then, Mrs. Jameson."

"Are you kidding me?" Lila gasped.

"She wants cupcakes for a small affair at her house." Amelia shook her head. "Right when her son-in-law is being laid to rest?"

"You know what? I don't think that's strange at all." Lila came to Luann's defense. "When your whole life is work-work-work, when a crisis hits, the only thing you know how to do is stay busy. That was how Jacob coped with my cancer."

"You're right." Amelia nodded. "But I think I might stop by the wake. Maybe."

"It wouldn't be the wildest thing anyone did."

The next day, the details for the wake of Gregory Timber Scottson were listed in the Gary Bugle. Amelia showed up at the Brockheim Funeral Home and lingered in the back of the room.

I shouldn't have come to this. She smoothed the nape of her neck. *I don't know these people.* But when she looked at the front of the room, she saw Colleen sitting alone. No one was talking to her or offering their condolences, even though the room had a fair number of people in it.

Just then, Amelia saw Luann. She came sweeping into the room, wearing a rather low-cut black wrap-around dress that left very little to the imagination. Her long blond hair was pulled back in a tight ponytail, and she was leading a very young, handsome fellow into the room behind her.

"Colleen, you remember Roger?" Amelia heard her mother say.

Colleen didn't say anything.

"Colleen, you look really beautiful," Roger gushed. It was obvious he couldn't take his eyes off Colleen, but he was keenly aware he was at a funeral.

"Why don't you and Roger go talk? Get some

fresh air," Luann urged.

"I don't want to talk!" Colleen shouted. "I don't want any fresh air! I want Greg back!"

She sounded so young, Amelia's heart broke for the girl. It reminded her of the time Meg's first pet died. She was only six, and her pet was a smelly hamster that she named Napoleon. Amelia hated the thing, but Meg loved it. She had it for two years before the little guy just fell asleep. Meg was beside herself.

"I just want to walk in my room and see him running on his wheel." Her baby sniffled.

But this wasn't a hamster. This was a husband. Amelia couldn't stand it. She watched Colleen stomp out of the room and waited for Luann to follow after her. But Luann didn't do that. Instead, she apologized to Roger and his parents, who were offering their condolences. Amelia couldn't take it and followed Colleen out the door, unnoticed. She found her sitting on a folding chair in an empty viewing room.

"Colleen?" Amelia whispered. "I don't know if you remember me."

"The Pink Cupcake." Colleen smiled prettily through running mascara and red eyes. "Yes, I remember you. It's so nice of you to come." She sniffed, stood, and offered her hand to Amelia, who shook it.

"I just wanted to say I was sorry for your loss. I know you don't know me, but I thought you and Greg made a lovely couple that time I spoke to the two of you, and since I'm having some cupcakes sent to your house tomorrow, I—"

"You're what?" A shadow fell over Colleen's eyes.

"Having cupcakes delivered to your house. Your mother ordered them. They are your favorites. The chocolate raspberry kind." Amelia felt like an inept kindergarten teacher trying to reason with a five-year-old. "She told me you liked those the best."

The cloud passed as quickly as it had surfaced, and again Colleen smiled politely.

"Yes. My mother is arranging the luncheon at our house. She said she was."

Amelia sensed uneasiness in Colleen's voice and was suddenly wishing she had talked herself out of coming.

"I could tell when your mother called that she was very worried about you," Amelia lied. "Some people just have a hard time getting it out. They make you look for the compassion with a fine-tooth comb. But rest assured, it's in there."

Colleen looked at Amelia as if she were getting directions.

"That's very kind of you," Colleen said. "I know my mother means well. But I'm not like her. I'm more sensitive, like my dad." She sighed, and a fresh spring of tears welled up in her eyes. "I wish he were here."

Amelia plucked a Kleenex from a nearby table and handed it to Colleen, who blew her nose loudly.

"I'll leave you alone," Amelia said soothingly. She watched Colleen take her seat again, and when the girl didn't say anything else, Amelia took a step toward the door. That was when she saw the face peering in at them. A man had been eavesdropping.

Feeling her entire back bristle, Amelia took off after him. She saw a portly-looking guy in a wrinkled denim jacket and black slacks quickly stride down the hallway, to the lobby, and out the front door.

Are you really going to chase him down? Amelia thought for a split second. *Yes, I am.*

Without drawing too much attention to herself, Amelia pursued the strange man into the parking lot. He was fumbling with his keys when she saw him.

"Hey!" she shouted. "Hey, you! I want to talk to you!"

The man looked up and snickered.

"It's no big deal, lady. I didn't do anything."

"I didn't say you did," Amelia snapped back. "But your remark makes me think you might be up to no good."

"Oh, no. Not me. I'm the only one trying to do *any* good. I'm the only one who knows the truth, and no one will believe me."

"How do you know Colleen?"

The man bit his lip. He wouldn't be unattractive if he'd get his hair trimmed off his collar and maybe wear a pair of dress shoes instead of gym shoes with his slacks.

"I don't really know her," he muttered, looking up at the sky. He scratched his eyebrow. "I mean, I've just been her neighbor for over ten years. But her mother the pit bull never let the outside world infringe on her azaleas."

Could this be the rarely seen Bud Fetzer?

"I don't really know her either. My name is Amelia Harley." She extended her hand.

"Bud Fetzer," the man replied, looking down his nose at Amelia as if he were studying lobsters in a tank, looking for the healthiest specimen. His lips pulled down at the corners as though he smelled something bad.

"So Bud. Why were you eavesdropping on Colleen and me?"

"I wasn't eavesdropping. I was hoping I might be able to get her alone for just a minute."

"To do what?" Amelia's eyes flashed with that same storm she'd seen in Colleen's eyes.

"Please, don't get your panties in a bunch. It's nothing like that. Get your mind out of the gutter."

Amelia gasped.

"I needed to talk to her about something that I'm not sharing with you, Amelia Harley." Bud smirked. "It's a matter for law enforcement, if you must know."

"Law enforcement?" Amelia looked Bud up and down.

"For what it's worth. The law enforcement in Gary is hardly the public's first line of defense. If they knew what I knew. Let's just say more people would have those decorative bars on their doors and windows. But they want to stay blind. Asleep. But all you have to do is listen."

"Listen? To what?"

"My podcast." Bud pulled a card from his pocket and handed it to Amelia. Clock-watcher's

Report was written in black letters over a plain white background with nothing but Bud's name and an email address on it. "I've got over one million subscribers. Over a million people from all over the country are awake. But I can't get my neighbor to flipping open her eyes for even a second. Not even one second."

"Do you have a crush on Colleen?" Amelia asked kindly as if she were talking to Adam or someone his age.

"What?" Bud blushed. "No. I mean, she's beautiful. But she knows it. It's only a matter of time before she takes on her mother's personality and the whole fantasy is ruined."

"Fantasy?"

"Look, Amelia, I don't know what you want from me, but I'm getting out of here. There are eyes and ears all over the place. I have to watch my back. Now that you've been seen with me, you better do the same."

He climbed into a beautiful silver BMW and quickly zoomed out of the parking lot and onto the quiet street.

Before he hit the first traffic light, Amelia had Dan on the phone.

CHAPTER SIX

AFTER TELLING Dan what Bud had said to her, Amelia was on her way to relieve Lila of her duties for the day. She had graciously agreed to steer the ship until Amelia returned, and when she saw her face and a batch of burnt PB&J cupcakes, she felt a wave of guilt.

"I should have never left you alone," Amelia said, fretting, as she quickly dumped her purse and pulled on a pink apron.

"I'm sorry. We got slammed, and those PB and Js were the casualties. You know, when we first started, you could walk away from the truck for two hours and the steady stream was manageable. But now, you are in demand. How many magazines have you been written up in?"

"I lost count." Amelia grabbed a rag and started cleaning the workstation in order to start a new batch.

"So it's not a bad thing."

"That's it, Lila. Take a break. In fact, if you want to leave for the day, I'll handle the truck."

"What? And not hear what you learned at the Scottson funeral? No way."

Amelia chuckled and shook her head. The truth was she did learn a good deal at the Scottson funeral, and she repeated it to Lila, up to and including her call to Dan.

"You know, I hate to say it, but this little incident with Bud Fetzer has given me the jolt of energy I've been needing," Amelia confessed. "Lila, we need to hire an assistant. You write up the ad. Anyone with food truck experience will be bumped to the front of the line. Anyone with baking experience will be hired."

"You got it, boss lady. Now tell me, do you think that Bud Fetzer had something to do with Greg's death?"

"I don't know. He just didn't act right. Dan

always says go with your gut. That's why I called him."

"I went with my gut when I joined Rusty for a pig roast at his house. The whole pig was cooked in the ground."

"How is Rusty? You haven't mentioned him in a while." Amelia smiled. Rusty owned the Twisted Spoke biker bar and restaurant in town and was just as delightfully odd and brassy as Lila.

"He's off on his yearly sabbatical through Idaho and Montana."

"Yikes. He's looking for a little solitude."

"He says it keeps him centered and he remembers how small he is in the grand scheme of things."

"He didn't ask you to tag along?" Amelia winked.

"Actually, he did. Something about one sleeping bag and a blanket of stars over our heads every night."

Amelia stared at her friend.

"Amelia, do I look like the kind of girl who sleeps outside?"

Both ladies laughed just as Amelia's phone went off. It was Dan.

"I just came from Bud Fetzer's place," Dan reported. "We've got a bit of a problem."

"Did another camera fall on you?" Amelia asked seriously.

"Not quite. Bud took me into his house."

"Oh no. Did he make you watch reruns of *Star Trek* and *Doctor Who*?" Amelia teased. Quickly, she realized that Dan was not in a joking mood.

"He's got an arsenal of surveillance devices in there. Night-vision goggles. Infrared binoculars. He's got video surveillance cameras that connect with half a dozen television screens showing what's out there on his property. Telescopes that can focus in on a flea on a pinhead. It's at least a hundred thousand dollars' worth of equipment."

"That's quite a hobby," Amelia said.

"He's also got a telescope and two surveillance cameras that are pointed directly at the Jameson house."

"Eww." Amelia squealed. "See, I told you I got a slimy feel from the guy."

"Right. I asked him why he was watching them."

"What did he say?"

"As cool as a cucumber, he said he wasn't watching them. He was watching the northern sky since that was where SETI had reported a highly active area of the sky for unidentified flying objects."

"What in the world is SETI?"

"The Search for Extra-Terrestrial Intelligence," both Dan and Lila replied in unison. Amelia looked at Lila in surprise.

"So is he saying aliens did something to Greg?"

"Nope. He's saying he saw a man up on the roof."

"So he saw Greg up there?"

"He said he saw Greg up there and another man toss him off the roof."

Amelia slumped.

"I don't know what to say." Amelia hadn't been prepared for such an odd response. Instead, she thought about her visit tomorrow to the Jameson home for the funeral luncheon.

"Neither do I," Dan muttered. "We are required to follow up with every lead, but I don't know if this can be considered a lead. The guy sees shadow people and men in black and a conspiracy on every billboard and television ad. What am I supposed to do?"

Amelia heard the worry in Dan's voice.

"Do what you always tell me, Dan. Go with your gut."

"I was afraid you were going to say that."

Amelia chuckled.

They chatted for a few more minutes before Amelia hung up and looked at Lila, who was yawning.

"All right, young lady," Amelia snapped. "You go home. Get me that ad for an assistant for tomorrow, and we'll get some help in here."

"What is the pay?"

"What? We have to pay them?" Amelia joked. "We start off at minimum wage with an increase for good work in three months and bonuses."

Lila nodded, yawned again, stood from the stool she was perched on, and grabbed her purse.

"I'll have this for you tomorrow," she said with her mouth stretched open.

"Bring it by the house around four. I think we both need a sabbatical for one day from the truck."

Lila nodded and stepped off the truck while waving good-bye. Amelia set to baking a replacement batch for the PB&J cupcakes that had been burnt, and thought about Bud Fetzer.

The following morning, Amelia was up early and had the pleasure of working closely with her two favorite seasonal assistants, Adam and Meg.

"You don't ever have to worry about me, Mom," Meg piped up as she popped plain white paper cups into the muffin tins. "I'm not going to fall for some guy just because he's cute."

"He'd have to be blind, too, in order for him to fall for Meg," Adam teased.

"I did hear Amy was dropped on her head as a baby," Meg volleyed back. "That explains a lot. She probably only writes with crayons because she can't be trusted with sharp pens or pencils."

"All right. That's enough." Amelia rolled her eyes as she added an egg to the mixture she was beating.

"Meg's never going to date, anyway." Adam said. "That would take too much time away from her gabbing with Katherine over world events like crappy music and crappy movies and the crappy books they read."

"At least we know how to read and can do it in the daylight without worrying about shriveling up and turning to dust."

"Okay, you two," Amelia said. "We are not going to say anything mean about each other the rest of the morning, or else I'm going to have to go all psycho mom. Do you want that?"

"No, ma'am," both children replied in unison.

"Meg, I just thought we should discuss these things about boys now. Adam, you are no exception. There are people out there who are just looking to make themselves happy with money or whatever. I want you kids to judge people by how they treat you, not how they look or what they can give you."

"Is that what Jennifer did to Dad?" Adam asked.

The question froze Amelia to her bones.

Hell yes, that's what that home-wrecker did! She saw a meal ticket and latched on with both talons.

"I think they love each other, Adam." Amelia wanted to puke. "We just need to be happy for them, and if we can't be happy, we can be kind. Right?"

"She's nothing compared to you, Mom," Meg chirped as she grabbed another baking tin. "She doesn't even know how to cook."

"That's because she's so young." Okay, Amelia felt a little good getting in that jab.

"I'm young, and I know how to cook," Meg bragged.

"You do, angel. But don't ever cook so good your husband doesn't take you out for dinner." Amelia winked.

"Mom, are Dad and Jennifer going to have kids?" Adam seemed to be very interested in the workings of John and Jennifer's marriage. Amelia took a deep breath.

"Jennifer is young, and it is only natural that she's going to want to have kids too someday. So I wouldn't rule it out, but it might be a couple years yet before that happens. Why do you ask?"

"It's just been so hard growing up with Meg that I just don't know if I could do it again with a stepbrother or sister."

Amelia smiled, and Meg rolled her eyes.

"Luckily for you, I have primary custody of you kids, and so the sleepless nights of baby crying will be at a minimum. But look at it this way. If your dad and Jennifer do have a baby, I think you guys could take turns babysitting and make yourselves some cash."

Their eyes lit up, and they looked at each other.

"What do babysitters charge?" Meg asked.

Amelia arched an eyebrow.

"Oh, nowadays, I don't think your dad would be able to pay less than fifteen dollars an hour, and that would be for a stranger in their home. People will pay for security. You might get a little more."

"That's even more than you pay!" Meg squealed.

"Yeah, well, you won't get free cupcakes. You'll get dirty diapers. But I think you'd both make excellent babysitters."

Sure, it was petty, and John hadn't even talked about having kids, let alone hitting Adam or Meg up for babysitting duty. But Amelia didn't feel the least bit guilty for planting the expensive seed of babysitting fees. Especially since her ex-husband was on a crusade to give less and less as his new wife cost him more and more.

"Okay, Mom. These are ready for the batter," Meg said, setting the cupcake tins in an assembly line.

"Adam, how's that raspberry glaze coming along?"

"Mom, I could make this in my sleep. In fact, I think I did because you got us up so early."

"Yeah, Mom. You know Adam needs his beauty rest. But for it to do any good, he'd need to be in a coma."

"Meg, don't talk about your brother being in a coma. That's morbid."

"Yeah, Meg," Adam grumped.

"Adam, don't antagonize your sister." Amelia sighed as she spooned the mixture slowly into the cups. "I swear you two are going to make me start drinking."

"So how much are you getting paid for this job, Mom?" Adam asked.

"This is a good one. Due to the short notice, even though the quantity isn't huge, I think we'll get about five hundred dollars."

Adam and Meg's eyes lit up again.

"Mom, since I am the oldest, when you die, I get to inherit the business, right?"

"That's not fair. I work there more than you," Meg interrupted.

"That's only because you aren't in any after-school activities." Adam cleared his throat.

"Yeah, talking about computers at the Nerds Swap and Spit or whatever it's called makes you a real socialite."

"It's the Programmers Host and Hack. Get it right."

Amelia couldn't help laughing at Meg's jab. It was funny even if it was at her son's expense.

"I'm not dying anytime soon, so let's not talk about who gets my stuff. We need to get these cupcakes done, and they need to be perfect. This is a real tough customer. I have to make a good impression."

"Yes, ma'am," the kids once again chimed in unison. It was a beautiful morning. What could go wrong?

CHAPTER SEVEN

AMELIA COULD NEVER DRIVE through Sarkis Estates and not gasp and sigh at the beautiful homes. Some were just big and made her jaw drop. But others were made to really reflect the owners who lived in them. Not everyone had a giant copper sunflower or a bright-red vintage tractor in their yard. Some people had water fountains. Others had waterfalls that Amelia bet there were koi swimming around in along with a couple dozen copper pennies thrown in for fun.

But the Jameson home was not in the main area of Sarkis Estates. It was just close enough to the border of Brightway that there may have been a significant tax break. Amelia couldn't be sure. Brightway was an old neighborhood of people who were living out their golden years in ranch-style homes that were paid in full two decades earlier. They were middle class, plain and simple.

A natural divide of about an acre of wooded area and pine trees separated Sarkis Estates from the smaller, more conservative homes in Brightway.

Luann Jameson's house was a huge manor with four pillars across the front of the house. The yard was pristinely kept. Not a stray leaf or brazen weed creeping up on the lawn. The flowers were perfectly maintained and bloomed happily even on this day that was anything but happy for the people living in the house.

Amelia slowed the hot-pink truck down as she approached the house and saw what had to be Bud Fetzer's place. In contrast, his house was a beautifully rustic-looking home that almost blended in completely with the wooded landscape to the right and behind the house.

"That would be a breathtaking house if all the cameras and satellite dishes were removed and maybe the walkway was swept," Amelia said to herself. It looked as if curtains covered the windows on the first and second floor. But the third-floor windows were wide open, and three of those windows faced the Jameson home. Amelia shivered.

She pulled into the driveway at the Jameson house by a young man in skinny jeans and a plaid shirt buttoned all the way up his neck, who pointed down the extended driveway.

"Please pull around to the back to the service entrance," he chirped.

Amelia nodded and followed the driveway around to the back of the house. There were two other trucks there. One looked as if it was providing beverages. The other was the caterer for the lunch —Katie Pix Catering. Amelia had heard of her. She was the caterer for every political event in the city. Hopefully, she'd get to snag a plate of Katie's goodies for herself.

Another woman was waiting back there to assist Amelia.

"Just park over there, and we'll get the boys to bring in the cupcakes."

"Okay" was all Amelia could think to say.

Two large men in black pants and white shirts came up to the truck. Without anything more than a grin, Amelia handed them each a box of cupcakes. Grabbing one herself, she followed them inside.

They wove their way through what Amelia guessed was a mudroom of sorts. It was an absolutely sparkling, sweet-smelling mudroom for only the cleanest muddy boots. There were thick cream-colored towels stacked on shelves along with several umbrellas hanging from pegs. There wasn't a single scuff or smudge on the brown tiled floor.

The super-fancy mudroom opened up into a kitchen that would make Wolfgang Puck green with envy. As Amelia looked at all the steel appliances and marble countertops, she was once again struck by how sterile everything looked. It was beautiful. On her best day, Amelia couldn't get her kitchen to look this clean. She wondered if Luann or even a hired chef ever used this kitchen. If they did, they must have had a maid that had a real violent hatred of filth.

"Are those the desserts?" a third person asked Amelia. She was a blond-haired girl in a black skirt and a peach-colored blouse, carrying a clipboard and with a Bluetooth in her ear.

"Yes," she replied. "One hundred double-chocolate raspberry cupcakes from The Pink Cupcake."

"One hundred?" the woman snapped. "There were supposed to be one hundred and ten." She tapped her Bluetooth.

"No. Luann told me one hundred. I've got it written down. The price I quoted was for one hundred. It was all explained to her," I replied calmly.

Without looking at her, the woman indicated for Amelia to follow her into a room where the food was already being displayed. Amelia almost fainted. There was prime rib, lobster tails, and a vegetarian lasagna that was at least seven layers high. It smelled wonderful.

There was a small table where Amelia began to assemble the cupcakes. She went back to the truck to get the displays to stack the cupcakes on, making them look more like an artistic sculpture than just a bunch of cupcakes.

Bluetooth Woman had left, and Amelia decided to take this opportunity to have a look around. According to her watch, she had about ten minutes before the mourners were expected to arrive. This was one heck of a sendoff for Greg. Amelia looked around, hoping to see maybe a wedding picture of him and Colleen or maybe a picture at a family get-together. Strangely, there was nothing. In fact, there wasn't really anything to indicate that this was for a funeral. It looked like a fundraiser or perhaps a wedding brunch.

"Rich people are weird," Amelia grumbled before asking someone where the bathroom was.

Amelia made her way through the dining room, past a sitting room, to a lovely winding staircase. Once upstairs, she slowly walked down the hallway. There were lovely paintings on the walls and a couple of pictures of Colleen. High school graduation. College graduation. Luann and Colleen with the late Mr. Jameson, who was at least two decades older than Luann.

He wasn't the most handsome man Amelia had ever laid eyes on. Every man looked handsome in a suit and tie, but he did have a smile that even Amelia, as she looked at the picture, couldn't help but return. It was contagious.

Inching down the hallway, Amelia was careful to listen for anyone coming up behind her. She found the bathroom. But before slipping inside, she took a few more steps to peek into the bedrooms.

"This is crazy. You are going to get busted. Just go back downstairs. What could be up here?" she muttered. But that was when she saw that the first room on the right side of the hall looked like the room of a young woman.

"This must be Colleen's room. But if she was married, where did Greg sleep?" she asked the single bed with four posts. Another step inside the room, and Amelia saw an impeccably neat dresser and a desk with stationery on the blotter.

Out the window, through the lacy curtains, was a view of Bud Fetzer's place.

Even with the thin curtain distorting the view, Amelia still shuddered, thinking Bud was watching the place.

Just as she turned to leave the room, she saw the only thing that looked out of place—a packet of papers that were stapled together, sloppily bent and rolled as if someone had been worrying the corners. It was on the nightstand next to a facedown picture frame.

Quickly, Amelia tiptoed over to the nightstand and flipped over the photo. It was Colleen and Greg on their wedding day. Bright smiles were on their faces as they looked at each other. Colleen was a beautiful bride, and Greg really did clean up nicely. They looked like they fit together.

"That poor girl." Amelia put the frame back the way she found it. She picked up the documents, but what she saw caused her breath to hitch in her throat.

It was an insurance policy. On various pages were little red Post-it tabs with the words Sign Here on them.

Flipping through the pages, Amelia saw Gregory Timber Scottson was worth six million dollars dead.

"This is interesting."

But before she could set the paper down, she heard voices on the steps. One she was sure was Luann. Thinking fast, she dropped to the floor and rolled underneath the bed. Thankfully, Colleen had a neat room and nothing under her bed.

Amelia held her breath as Luann and Colleen walked into the room.

"Have you signed the papers yet?" Luann asked.

The papers? The papers! The papers that were still in Amelia's hand!

Brilliant, she scolded herself.

"Mom, he hasn't even been gone a week,"

Colleen whined. "I can't think about that stuff right now."

"Well, honey, you need to think about it. Where are they?"

Amelia watched her mother's fancy pumps walk over to the desk. Colleen's remained still by the dresser. With lightning speed, Amelia thrust the papers out from under the bed, leaving them on the floor by the nightstand.

"They're over here." Colleen walked over and without comment picked the insurance policy up from the ground.

"You haven't signed a single page," Luann snapped. "Look, I know you are mourning, and I know this hurts, but the sooner you can get this over with, the sooner we will be able to move on with our lives."

"Mom, the house is filling up with guests. I'm not going to look at this right now."

Colleen's flat ballet-slipper shoes turned and walked out the door. Luann's stood there. Amelia was sure the woman could see through the mattress and box spring and was watching her underneath the bed. Any second, she was going to drop down to her knees and yank up the bed sham and scream, "*A-ha!*"

But that didn't happen.

Luann dropped the papers back on the night-stand and left. Amelia let out the breath she hadn't known she was holding. Now she really and truly had to go to the bathroom. Giving Luann enough time to go back downstairs, Amelia shimmied out from underneath the bed like a crab escaping a seagull and darted on tiptoe across the hallway to the bathroom.

That made her gasp as well. The tiles on the floor looked like smooth stones from a Zen garden, and they climbed the walls in the shower and along the backsplash of the double sink. A sunk-in tub with eight different jets in it sat beneath a small stained-glass window that allowed the light in but obstructed any view in or out.

The soaps were little lavender balls, and the mirrors were beveled, with elaborate scrolling around the edges. The towel rack was heated.

"For heaven's sake." Amelia shook her head as she washed her hands and darted back downstairs.

Colleen was right. As she tried to maneuver her way back the way she had come, Amelia was forced to take a couple of weird turns and pass through unfamiliar rooms where people were talking and hugging and visiting. She swore it took an additional ten minutes to get her bearings and arrive back at her table in the dining room.

After letting out a deep breath, she pulled a couple of business cards from her pocket and set them in front of her lovely cupcake display and stood back while the guests helped themselves.

CHAPTER EIGHT

WHEN AMELIA HAD BEEN HIDING under the bed, all she could see from her hiding place under the bed were Luann's shoes. But when she saw her entire ensemble, she had to fight not to stare. The dress reminded Amelia of the character Elvira, Mistress of the Night, who would run all those bad horror movies. Every curve was showing, and her cleavage was on full display.

Maybe she can't help it? Amelia wondered as she watched her spend a few moments with each one of her guests. *Maybe that's how all of her clothes fit her and there isn't anything she can do about it.* She looked at the faces of the guests and wondered if they were as shocked as she. But aside from the casual glance of a gentleman or two, no one seemed to notice Luann's outfit.

Colleen walked in and was a stark contrast to her mother. She wore a lovely black business suit. She reciprocated a couple hellos as she fixed herself a small plate of cheeses, bread, and some grapes.

"I'm going to go sit in the kitchen," Amelia heard her tell her mother. Luann mumbled something, but Colleen shrugged her off. "I'm going to sit in the kitchen," she said loud enough to get her point across.

Luann let her arms flop to her sides as she shook her head.

"I just don't know what I'm going to do with that girl." Luann pouted her lips at a sympathetic guest who was standing nearby.

"Just give her some time, Lu. She'll come around," the man said, sidling up to Luann.

"She blames herself," Luann replied, looking at the man and then at Amelia, who was within earshot. "I keep telling her that she couldn't have known what Greg was going to do while she was gone. They had been struggling."

"Is that so?" the man asked, obviously enjoying Luann's attention and probably the view as well.

"Greg, well, he wasn't making enough money

at the garage for them to move out the way they had planned. His heart was in the right place. Believe me. I could see it." Luann nodded in Amelia's direction. "But he just didn't have the ambition. He started smoking, you know, marijuana."

"Oh, that is too bad. It is a gateway drug, they say," the man said encouragingly.

Amelia said nothing and didn't move.

"I had been complaining that the roof needed a few tiles replaced. If anyone should blame themselves, it should be me." She sort of sobbed. Amelia noticed she *sort of* did. "Colleen was at the salon. I had made an appointment for her with my stylist. The girl was running a little behind with her client, so Colleen had to wait. She hadn't had her hair done in so long, and I was treating her to a manicure. It was supposed to be a beautiful day. But I forgot my wallet."

The man nodded, never taking his eyes away from Luann's face.

"It's probably a blessing that I did. Had Colleen been the one to find him... My God. She would have died right there on the spot next to him. I know she would have."

Colleen hadn't seen the accident. No one was

home when it happened. Amelia wondered if he could have been saved if someone had been home.

"Greg thought he would do me a favor and climb up on that roof and fix those loose shingles for me. I would have never let him do it if I'd known that was his plan. He was trying to earn his keep the only way he knew how. Using his hands. Let's face it, he wasn't valedictorian like Colleen was."

"Colleen has inherited that from you, Luann. But somehow she has Walter's heart."

"He's raised her since she was eight. It's amazing how much of him I see in her, and they don't share a single drop of blood."

Amelia had no idea the late Mr. Jameson was not Colleen's real father. She wondered who was.

"Does her real father know what happened? Have you spoken to him?" the man asked as if reading Amelia's mind.

"Burt? Burt can't be bothered. He's not even in the state anymore. For all I know, he isn't in the country. When I married, child support was no longer an issue. He pulled up stakes, and I've not heard from him in well over ten years now."

"That's too bad."

"It is for Colleen. Not me." Luann chuckled.

"The only good thing to come out of that arrangement was my beautiful daughter."

"Colleen needs you now. She needs you to be strong for her," the man continued. "Like you always are."

"You're right, Hank. But sometimes, sometimes I really wish someone was there to be strong for me."

"If there is anything I can do for you, anything at all, day or night, just call me."

"Thank you, Hank. Please tell Dolores I said thank you, too."

The man kissed Luann on the cheek then turned to the buffet and continued to load his plate.

"It's a sad business," Luann continued talking to Amelia.

"It is. I'm sorry for your loss, Mrs. Jameson."

"Well, we don't get out of this world alive, do we?" She smirked.

"No. I guess we don't."

"Cherish the people you love." Luann nodded. "That's the most important thing."

She grabbed one of Amelia's cupcakes and a napkin and skated out of the room as if she were floating instead of walking.

By the time the luncheon was over, Amelia

didn't have a single cupcake left, and all of her business cards were gone. As she disassembled the displays, Luann appeared with the Bluetooth girl.

"There seems to be a bit of a problem," Luann stated. The woman who seemed so delicate earlier, who fretted over her poor daughter, was gone.

The first thing to come to Amelia's mind was that maybe her truck was parked wrong and she was blocked in or that perhaps she shouldn't have put her business cards out.

"You didn't complete the order as I had requested," Luann snapped with a smirk on her red lips.

"I'm sorry," Amelia stammered. "What?"

"I specifically ordered one hundred and ten cupcakes. You arrived with only one hundred."

"With all due respect, Mrs. Jameson, I have the receipt right here. I spoke to you directly on the phone and repeated the order more than once to…"

"Look, I'm just not going to pay for a job that wasn't done."

"The job was done. I was here on time, and I provided one hundred cupcakes per your instructions." Amelia remained calm on the outside.

"In fact, I'll be contacting my lawyer. On the day of my son-in-law's funeral, you caused additional anxiety to my family and guests. This is unacceptable."

"Is this a joke?" Amelia looked at the woman with the Bluetooth in her ear, who stood there looking smug.

"If you take your little cupcake business as a joke, Mrs. Harley." Luann waved her hand at Amelia as if she were waving away a fly. "Like I'm sure most people do. I'm certainly not laughing. I'm humiliated, quite frankly. Now, please leave my home."

Amelia's mouth hung open.

"You owe me my money. I'm not leaving until you pay me for services rendered." Amelia folded her arms across her chest.

"Bridgette, call the police," Luann ordered, making the Bluetooth woman jump to life.

"This is ridiculous, Mrs. Jameson. You know you told me one hundred cupcakes."

"Are you calling me a liar?"

"I'm saying that under the circumstances, maybe you aren't thinking clearly. As for my business, I built it up to what it is with my own hands without any help. Certainly a woman who has made a name for herself in her own business like you have can appreciate that."

What Amelia meant to be a compliment and a commonality that could bring them together back-fired. At the mention of Luann's business, the woman scowled.

"How dare you!" she hissed.

Amelia squinted as if she was trying to see what Luann had seen that would make her so mad. But there was nothing there.

"You get out of my house right now!"

Amelia sighed. Grabbing her display and tucking it under her arm, she went back through the kitchen, the spotless mudroom, and out onto the driveway, where her truck was waiting. The hired servants were standing around and staring at her. She couldn't tell if it was with pity or amusement.

She stored her fixtures in the back of the truck. Just as she was about to climb in and screech out of there, she heard something.

"Miss! Miss, wait!"

She turned to see Colleen running after her. Amelia hadn't seen her but the one time at the luncheon. Her eyes were still red, but they were bright and kind. Nothing like her mother's.

"Here. This should cover everything." She handed Amelia six hundred dollars. "Your cupcakes were delicious."

"Colleen, thank you. I'm afraid it might get you into trouble. I've dealt with tough customers before. Your mother is probably just stressed."

"No offense, miss, but you've never dealt with my mother." Amelia couldn't tell if it was with pride or fear that Colleen uttered those words. But it did feel like a warning of sorts. "Please, take the payment. It's all right, really."

Amelia took the money and stuffed it into her pocket.

"Come by my truck at Food Truck Alley," Amelia replied softly. "I'll buy you a cupcake and a coffee."

"That sounds nice. I'll try." Colleen glanced over her shoulder at the house as if looking for spying eyes. She reached out and shook Amelia's hand without another word then turned and hurried back into the house.

Without wasting a moment, Amelia hopped in the truck and peeled out of the driveway, leaving the Jameson estate. She was determined to never go back.

But before she could escape Sarkis Estates, she saw a man at the edge of the road, frantically waving her down. It was Bud Fetzer.

"You want the Illuminati to spot you coming

two miles away, don't you?" he criticized, scowling at the bright truck.

"I do," Amelia snapped. "What do you want? Are you hurt or something?"

"I wanted to know if you saw him in there." He jerked his head toward the Jameson house.

"Saw who?" Amelia's right eyebrow arched.

"The killer."

"Bud, that was the funeral luncheon for Greg. There was no one but family and friends there."

"Right. You know all this because you are so tight with the Jamesons." Bud's sarcasm was annoying. "Look. I know what you're thinking. You think that I'm just some lonely geek who posts conspiracy theories on Facebook all day. That is, when I'm not downloading X-rated videos. You think I'm obsessed with Colleen Jameson and that I'm more of a threat to her than the people she lives with."

"Close. Yeah," Amelia replied.

"Well, you, like the rest of the people in this isolated, sleepy little town, are wrong. Care to have your mind blown?"

"What are you talking about?"

"Pull this monster under the tarp, and I'll show you."

"Wait. I'm just a lady who sells cupcakes. Why do you think I can help you?"

"Right. Just a lady who sells cupcakes." Bud chuckled. "There have been over twenty-two murders in Gary this year. A Detective Dan Walishovski has responded to several of them. Your name has shown up on several of the police reports as a witness of sorts."

"How do you know that?" Amelia was shocked, but her gut was telling her she didn't need to be scared. In fact, she realized she was more scared of Luann than she was of Bud Fetzer.

"Don't worry, Mrs. Harley. Your secrets are safe with me." He narrowed his eyes. "Are mine safe with you?"

CHAPTER NINE

"I LIKE DETECTIVE WALISHOVSKI," Bud said as he led Amelia into his domicile. "He's a smart man."

"Yes, he is," Amelia concurred as she carefully stepped inside.

"Don't worry, Mrs. Harley. You're safe here. Would you like a cup of tea?"

Amelia looked around and was shocked at the level of electronics everywhere.

"This place looks like NORAD."

"Thank you!" Bud gushed. "That is quite a compliment coming from a civilian. Do you take your tea with sugar or cream?"

"Neither."

"Aha! A woman after my own heart. I like the hard stuff, too."

Bud shuffled ahead of Amelia down a well-lit hallway to the kitchen. It was a beautiful room with a long oak picnic table in the middle that looked like something Vikings or perhaps King Arthur's court would have used if the round table were unavailable. Antique bureaus and china cabinets graced the walls. An authentic wood-burning stove stood against the far wall with several cords of wood stacked next to it. The wallpaper was a pretty design of ribbon and flowers on a forest-green background. The only electronics in this room was a shortwave radio on the table.

The windows were also not covered, and the back door appeared to be unlocked.

"For a guy who claims they are all out to get you, how come this room is so open?"

"It's a false front," Bud admitted proudly. "If anyone made it past my security system, and that is highly unlikely, they would no doubt circle the house. When they find they can't see in the front, they'll search for a window they can see in. It's a simple, homey kitchen with tea on the burner and peanut butter and jelly in the cupboard. If they are still determined to get in, they'll find themselves trapped. Not unlike high-end jewelry stores."

"Am I trapped in here?" Amelia suddenly felt her pulse race as the color drained from her face.

"Of course not," Bud assured her. "Mrs. Harley, I need your help. I'm not out to hurt anyone. I'm only after the truth. Whether it's about the alien bases at Roswell or the MK Ultra experiments that are still going on or the murder that took place at the house next door."

"You're convinced Greg was murdered."

"That's what I told Dan when I spoke with him the other day."

"Do you have any proof?"

Bud looked at Amelia as he filled the teakettle with water from the tap of a farm-style kitchen sink.

"If my cameras hadn't been knocked down the day before the accident."

Amelia didn't say anything.

"You have to understand that I don't just have security cameras. I've got state-of-the-art surveillance cameras. Each one costs almost a thousand dollars. You can bet I know how to install them properly. For one to fall or get damaged would take a tall ladder and a sledge hammer."

Amelia thought of Dan's bandaged head and

busted arm. That camera hadn't been secured very well. But Amelia didn't say anything.

"But aside from that, I have these." He pointed to his eyes.

"What were you doing that you saw someone on the roof of the Jameson house?" Amelia wasn't sure she should be asking Bud any questions. If she backed him into a corner about things he couldn't answer, she might get herself in trouble.

"Okay, this will take a little explaining." Bud sighed as he put the kettle on the stove. He looked at Amelia intently, as if he were about to diagnose her with some incurable disease.

He rubbed his hands together then began.

"Fifteen months ago at 11:47 a.m. every day for seven consecutive weeks at the coordinates of 42.5559 latitude and -122.7813 longitude, an unidentified sphere would appear in the sky and hover for approximately 8.239 seconds before disappearing."

Amelia was shocked. But she wasn't sure what she was more shocked at: the fact that she was being told of a consistent UFO sighting or the fact that she was in Bud Fetzer's kitchen, waiting on a cup of tea.

"Those coordinates just happen to fall in the

line of view with the Jameson house. I'm looking at what would be at least four inches above their roof from the view of my telescope."

"So you admit that you have a telescope pointing toward their house. Toward Colleen's window."

"You really do have a dirty mind, Mrs. Harley."

"Look, you expect me to believe that you aren't spying on that poor girl?"

"Poor girl? That's an interesting choice of words." Bud shook his head as if Amelia had proven herself to be the average dolt he thought she was. "I'll have you know, Mrs. Harley, that I have a girlfriend. In fact, this Christmas, I plan on proposing."

"Let me guess. She lives in Canada."

"Of course not. She lives at 191st and LaGrange Road. She's an assistant at the Gary veterinarian's office. Her name is Fiona. Now, can we get back to the murder? Or do you want to know more about my personal life?"

Amelia chuckled and nodded for Bud to continue.

"I haven't seen this orb, sphere, whatever you want to call it in a few months, but every day, I check and log my results. So I was at my telescope at the precise time of the previous sightings, and that was when the movement below my line of vision caught my attention."

The teakettle began to whistle.

Amelia watched Bud fill two mugs. One was in the shape of the head of Mr. Spock from *Star Trek*, and the other was a UFO over some trees with the words The Truth is Out There stamped on it. Bud gave that one to Amelia and kept Spock's head for himself. He took a wooden box off the counter and set it on the table. Flipping it open, he revealed a dozen lovely tea choices.

Amelia looked up at him and gave Bud a sly smirk.

"May I suggest the golden oolong morning? It's robust yet not overwhelming."

Amelia couldn't help it. Regardless of a couple of questions and inconsistencies, she couldn't help but like Bud. He was the weirdest person she'd ever met. But she liked him and followed his suggestion with the golden oolong morning tea. He did the same.

"So that day I missed the 8.239 seconds because I saw a man on top of the roof. I couldn't understand what he was doing since he didn't have any tools or anything with him. But then I saw the other man."

Amelia held the warm mug in her hands, but a chill spread over her as she watched Bud's face. The color drained.

"The second man had a gun. He was pointing it at the first guy, who stood there with his hands up. He was helpless on that sloped roof."

"You didn't think to call the police right away?"

"Mrs. Harley, I have trespassers and vandals all the time. But because of my line of work, everyone assumes I'm crazy. Paranoid. I see things. But I'm not crazy."

"So what did you do?"

"I remained calm and thought if I'm not hallu-cinating, it will be on my surveillance camera because just in case I'm away, I have a camera trained on those coordinates. But as I said, someone had taken that camera out. I knew I wasn't seeing things."

"What happened then?" Amelia sipped her tea. "Oh, this is delicious."

"Told you." Bud nodded and sipped from his own cup. He let the tea go down, and then he looked at the tabletop. "I was sure the second man was going to shoot the first. But he didn't. He walked up to him and slugged him across the face. The man crumpled in a heap. Then the second man kicked him off the roof."

Amelia suddenly couldn't taste anything. When she looked at Bud, he had tears in his eyes.

"I've seen a lot of things, Mrs. Harley. But I never saw a man murdered." He swallowed hard then took a big gulp of tea, letting the hot water scald his throat to burn away the urge to cry.

"You told all this to Detective Walishovski?"

"I did." Bud nodded. "He said he'd look into it, and trust me, I do know these things take time."

"So what do you think I can do about it? You've told me all this, and now what?"

"Luann Jameson has a restraining order on me."

"What? Bud, why didn't you tell me that?"

"Because you'd assume it was because I was some pervy Peeping Tom when that isn't it. She's suing me for a fence that she claims is on her property. When I went to measure and confirm the property line, she said I was stalking her and that I was a threat. She claimed my cameras are recording her and her daughter. Let's face it. Luann knows what she looks like, and she knows what I look like. Who are they going to believe?"

"Her," I mumbled.

"Yup. So I can't get within five hundred feet of her."

"So why were you at the funeral? You could have been thrown in jail."

"I was hoping I could talk to Colleen. I wanted to tell her what I saw. But you were there swapping recipes for hours on end. I couldn't wait and risk being seen."

"Still, you haven't told me what you expect me to do about it."

"The guy on the roof had a mask on. But he was young and muscular. And whoever he was knew Luann."

"How do you know that?"

"Because when he climbed down off the ladder, she was waiting for him."

Amelia didn't know what to think. Her mouth went completely dry. She took another sip of tea and cleared her throat.

"Amelia, you need to find that guy."

"Based on the suggestion of a guy who has a restraining order, who watches the skies for UFOs and lives in a virtual bunker, trying to stay one step ahead of the men in black."

"That's right." He sipped his tea and smiled.

CHAPTER TEN

"THAT'S QUITE A STORY," Dan muttered. "Bud didn't tell me about the restraining order. I found out about that when I looked into his background."

"There's also his claim about being an expert at putting up the cameras but one fell on you," Amelia added. She tucked her legs beneath her after taking a sip of wine and snuggling closer to Dan on her couch. "So what do you think?"

Dan took a sip and stretched his arm behind Amelia.

"I might go visit Bud again. You said you had tea with him?"

"Yes, it was quite delightful. Considering we

were discussing surveillance cameras and strangers climbing on roofs and murder."

"Plus, Luann Jameson threatened to sue you over what again?"

"Ten cupcakes," Amelia stated flatly.

"Sounds like you had a very interesting day."

"To say the least. I kind of wish the kids weren't at their friends' houses tonight. I would have liked to hear the plain and simple high school gossip about this popular girl or that jock or the teacher who smells like butter."

"Do they have a teacher who smells like butter?" Dan asked, as if this were a major concern.

"I don't know. There is always some teacher who smells like something, real or imagined. Isn't there? Usually one of the not-so-popular teachers."

"I don't remember any that smelled, but I did have a teacher who chronically picked his nose," Dan offered proudly.

"Eww. I could have gone the rest of my life not hearing that."

"It could have been worse."

"How?" Amelia shook her head. "Wait. Don't tell me. I think the worst I can remember is Miss Sleeve. She always had spit in the corners of her mouth. She was a nice lady, but it was hard not to focus on the spit when talking to her."

"Now look at us." Dan scoffed. "Little did we know the Miss Sleeves of the world would turn out to be normal compared to some of the people we've encountered."

Amelia giggled.

They finished their wine, and Dan promised he would let her know what he found out on his visit to Bud's place. He adjusted his arm that was still in a sling.

"Be careful," Amelia said as she smoothed his lapel. "Just because he served tea doesn't mean he might not be unstable, and you are about as ready for a fight as a one-legged man in a butt-kicking contest."

"Thanks."

"Just giving it to you straight, Detective." She looked up at him lovingly. "My way of saying be careful."

Dan looked down at her, and she felt the jitters in her chest when he winked.

A couple of kisses later, Dan was in his car, heading home, and Amelia was grabbing her purse to head to the store and get some milk and eggs.

After getting her supplies, she contemplated

grabbing some fast food for herself, but before she could decide, she slammed on the brakes and almost screamed.

"I know that car!" She gasped, her heart pumping madly in her throat. "Where are you going in such a hurry?"

Luann Jameson drove a red Lexus with REALS on the license plate for her real estate business. Amelia was sure Luann didn't intentionally cut her off. She had no way of knowing Amelia drove an old sedan.

"Don't take it personally, Amelia. It's her road, and she needs to get where she's going. You're just a minor inconvenience."

Amelia watched the Lexus zoom ahead. Without thinking, Amelia hit the gas and began to follow.

Stop signs were just suggestions. Yellow lights meant go faster. Wherever Luann was headed, she was in a real hurry. But Amelia kept the car in sight and was surprised that after fifteen minutes of a high-speed tail, the Lexus pulled into the Four Seasons Hotel parking lot.

"This is interesting," Amelia muttered. She knew that John had several meetings a year at this particular hotel. She also knew it was one of the places he'd taken Jennifer to before the whole sordid affair came into the light. John was still a face recognized by some of the managers.

Keeping a safe distance, Amelia watched Luann drop the car with the valet. As usual, she was dressed like a pin-up model, and all eyes were on her as she sashayed into the lobby.

Amelia didn't want to tip the valet, so she parked her car. Carefully, she walked up to the revolving doors and looked in the lobby. Luann was nowhere to be seen, so Amelia entered.

"Did she go to a room?" Amelia pondered. "I could ask at the front desk. That would be pretty ballsy. But maybe I'm feeling ballsy. She did cut me off, after all."

Squaring her shoulders, Amelia strode up to the check-in desk.

"Hi. I was wondering if a friend of mine had checked in yet. Is there a reservation for Luann Jameson?"

The man behind the counter was very tall and thin, and it was obvious he didn't like having to wear a tie, as he continually tugged at his collar.

"I'm sorry. Can you spell that name for me?"

Amelia spelled it out, but the man shook his

head and said there was no reservation under that name.

"She must have checked in under her friend's name, and I don't know how to spell it. I'm just going to wait in the lobby. Thanks."

"Sure. You might want to enjoy a drink in our Signature Bar. It's just around the elevator bank to the right."

"Thanks. I think I will." Amelia smiled. If Luann went to a room, Amelia was out of luck. But maybe she'd hang around for a little while and see what happened.

The Signature Bar was an elegant room. It had dark wood along the bar and several tall table and stools scattered around the room. Along the far wall were much more intimate tables for two that were like scalloped clamshells, allowing their occupants to sit intimately close to one another.

In one of those cozy seats, Amelia saw the back of Luann's long blond mane. She was by herself. Amelia quickly glided as close to the booth as she could without being noticed and took a seat perched high up on a stool at one of the tall tables.

She watched the back of Luann's head, and it looked to Amelia as if she was texting on her phone. Every man who walked by looked at her, but she didn't seem to notice. She had to be extremely used to it by now.

Just then, a guy came stomping in, wearing tight-fitting jeans and a Harley-Davidson T-shirt. He looked completely out of place among the starched white collared shirts and crisp polos the other men were wearing. Even the waitstaff was dressed better.

"Hi. Welcome to Signature Bar." Speaking of waitstaff. The toothy waiter shocked Amelia out of her surveillance mode and made her jump. "I'm sorry. I didn't mean to shock you." He chuckled pleasantly. "My name is Pi. I'll be your server. Can I start you off with some water or perhaps a cocktail?"

"Hi, Pi," Amelia said awkwardly. "Um, I'd like a water and a menu, please."

"Absolutely, coming right up."

Amelia picked up the drink card that was underneath the pretty crystal votive candleholder on the table and held it slightly in front of her face while she studied Luann.

The shabby young man flopped into the booth across from her with a greasy smile on his face. He wasn't ugly, but he had sort of an oily sheen to him that made Amelia wince.

"Waiting long?" she heard him ask. She couldn't hear Luann's answer, but judging from the guy's reaction, Luann was not impressed.

"What are you talking about?" He leaned in toward Luann. "You didn't seem to have a problem with it before." He licked his lips.

"Here's your water and a menu," Pi interrupted again. "I see you've had a chance to look at our drink menu."

"I'd just like a couple more minutes," Amelia smiled pleasantly.

"Sure, take your time. I'll be back."

Pi whisked away like a feather on a breeze. Amelia looked down and saw a cosmopolitan on the drink menu. It was twenty-one dollars.

"They've got to be out of their minds," she mumbled before putting the small drink menu down and swapping it out for the larger food menu. She peeked over the top, still watching Luann and her guest.

"No one has said anything to me," the man answered. "No one has called."

Then Luann said something.

"I'm positive. Lu, you're just being a little too paranoid. The hard part is over."

Amelia leaned even farther toward Luann's

booth. Of course what she was hearing sounded dubious. Of course this stud was talking about land-scaping or refurbishing or some other custodial project. It was only from hanging around Bud all afternoon that it sounded like murder.

"Babe, it's done. Now, what do we do next?"

The stool Amelia was sitting on was just too far away. She'd have to take the booth next to Luann's in order to hear her, and that was just too risky. As she thought of her next move, she didn't realize she was staring right at Luann's companion.

He looked her straight in the eye then let his gaze blatantly feel her up. He smirked and gave her a greasy wink. It wasn't anything like Dan's wink. Not even close.

But Amelia blushed. Not from the wink but from embarrassment. What was worse was that the man seemed to enjoy it. But Luann didn't. She whirled her head around and clenched her teeth.

With all the drama of one of Meg's classmates, Luann pushed herself out of the booth and stomped up to Amelia.

Fearing the worst, Amelia picked up her glass of water and took a long gulp then set it out of Luann's reach.

"How funny to see you here." Luann snarled.

"Todd, this is the woman I told you about. She owns the Pink Cheesecake or something. Totally ruined Greg's luncheon." She started to get choked up. "A businesswoman taking advantage at a funeral luncheon. There is no name for it."

Amelia's heart was racing. What did this woman expect her to do? Did she want to fight? Was this going to have to move outside?

"Don't worry, Luann. Your daughter paid your bill for you," Amelia replied with as much kindness as she could muster. "As far as I'm concerned, the matter is closed."

Judging from Luann's response, Amelia knew that she had no idea Colleen had done this. The tears managed to stop rather quickly.

By now, the entire bar was staring at them as though they were watching a hornet buzz around, waiting to see who it would sting first.

"You need to quit following me, Mrs. Harley!" Luann shouted. "It's really pathetic."

"Miss, is this woman bothering you?" a man in a lovely gray suit and name tag that read "Nigel Frange, Manager" asked Luann.

"Are you kidding?" Amelia choked. She was at least a whole foot shorter than Luann and wasn't the one who started shouting.

"Ma'am, I'm afraid I'm going to have to ask you to leave," Nigel said before Luann could properly answer him.

"You're asking me to leave?" Amelia almost laughed. She couldn't control the smile of disbelief on her face. Wait until she told the kids their mom got tossed out of the Four Seasons Hotel. "This woman approached me."

"I'm sorry, ma'am, you need to leave." Nigel took a step toward Amelia while Luann stood behind him for safety reasons, of course.

"Fine." Amelia was mortified that everyone was looking at her, yet she felt like a rebel. She'd never been thrown out of a place before. Plus, the fact that her ex-husband still utilized the hotel and would probably find out about this made it even more exciting. For a second, she contemplated knocking her glass to the floor or kicking over her chair. But she changed her mind.

Keeping it classy, Amelia.

She walked out of the Signature Bar and out of the Four Seasons lobby with Nigel trailing close behind. Once outside, she fished in her small bag for her keys when she noticed a Harley-Davidson motorcycle parked near the front entrance. The license plate read TODD.

"There are no coincidences," Amelia said to herself as she wrote down a quick description of the bike and the plate name. "I should go buy myself a lottery ticket. It might be my lucky night."

She never imagined getting thrown out of a five-star hotel would be lucky, but she sure felt it. Luann was definitely up to something. That guy was the complete opposite of the man who was in all those pictures on the wall. His hands were permanently dirty. That Harley was not new and looked as if it had seen its fair share of Sturgis weekends. Plus, it had a set of metallic men's testicles hanging from the hitch. Talk about keeping it classy.

It was also a polar opposite for Luann's Lexus. Yes, Luann and Todd were as odd a pair as Colleen and Greg were. But up close, Colleen and Greg looked happy. She wasn't dragging him into an environment that he didn't fit in like a silk hat on a pig.

Turning around, she saw Nigel The Manager talking on a cell phone, staring out of the glass lobby windows at her. Nigel The Manager sounded like a pitiful superhero name. But his superpower was probably summoning the police with one quick call, so she hurried to her car and left.

On the way home, she called Dan but got his voicemail.

"Hi. It's me. Well, my night was just as thrilling as my day. Call me when you get a chance, and I'll tell you all about it."

CHAPTER ELEVEN

"WAIT A SECOND." Lila looked wide eyed at Amelia. "I know that guy."

"You know Luann Jameson's Todd? How?" Amelia gasped as she finished adding the glaze and one giant almond to the top of her apricot-walnut cupcakes.

"That bike you described is parked at Rusty's several times a month. Rusty doesn't like him. His full name is Todd Coz."

"Really? Why not?"

"As if the testicles on the back of his bike weren't enough. Rusty said he's one of those guys that no matter what story you tell, he's got one better. No matter what it is. He's a know-it-all." Lila took a drink of water. "He's been in prison a couple of times. A lot of those bikers have. But unlike normal ex-cons, Todd likes to relive the stories that got him sent there. He likes to see people's reactions. According to Rusty, he talks way too much. So how many of his yarns are factual is anyone's guess. But no one likes a guy who doesn't know when to keep his mouth shut."

"So there's a chance he might be at the Twisted Spoke."

"I'd say it's a pretty good bet. He's more likely to show up when Rusty isn't there because, well, you know how Rusty is. He won't put up with some blowhard disturbing his customers." Lila smiled devilishly.

"You really like that Rusty, don't you. Talk about complete opposites." Amelia winked.

"We aren't really all that different." Lila looked off in the distance. "He's really just a scruffier version of my ex-husband. He's ambitious and financially secure and has a charm about him that is darn near irresistible."

"Irresistible?" Amelia teased. "Why, Lila, you really are twitterpated. Do you miss him?"

"Not enough to sleep on the ground for him.

But yes. I can't wait until he gets back. It'll be about two or three more weeks."

"Ever think that maybe you might like to be Mrs. Rusty Twisted Spoke?"

Lila laughed.

"I don't think so. I'm having too much fun being Lila Bergman."

"Well, Lila Bergman, since we have to wait for Dan before we can make any moves, how about we go over that job description."

"Yes, one of my finest works thus far," Lila joked as she grabbed her bag and pulled out a folder. "In my spare time, I typed up a rules and regulations sheet, dress code, our views on firearms in the workplace…"

"What?"

"Don't worry, I had my lawyer look over it. It's all legal."

"You worry me sometimes, Lila." Amelia looked her friend up and down. "Do you have a weapon on you right now?"

"See, it's the wondering that makes them think twice. Always keep them guessing, Amelia. That goes for love and war."

In between another delightfully busy day, the ladies ironed out the ad that Amelia would have Adam upload to whatever job sites most applied to people searching for work on a food truck. Dan called back and said he'd meet Amelia after work to discuss what she was talking about in the message she left him the previous night.

"Well, another day in the black, Amelia." Lila smiled as she finished the receipts for the night. "I'll take these to the bank tonight. You said Dan was meeting you here?"

"Yeah. He said he'd be here in about an hour. I've got some scrubbing to do, so I'll be busy until he gets here," Amelia replied as she scrubbed the counter and sprayed it with disinfectant. "I'd appreciate your dropping off the bag. Tomorrow, the ad will be posted, so hopefully we will have a couple decent people to pick from."

"I'll keep my fingers crossed. You want me to wait with you until Dan shows up?"

"No. Go on home. We'll have a busy day tomorrow. I'll need you to run the truck while I sleep in the front seat," Amelia joked.

The last few things to be cleaned were the last batch of cupcake tins, and a slew of paper boats needed to be folded and ready for the next day.

Amelia liked being in the truck at closing time. It was quiet, with just the sounds of a couple of the other vendors talking quietly and maybe a few stragglers weaving their way through the park on their way home.

It was at times like this Amelia would have liked a glass of wine and a good book. She could easily sit at the counter with the heat from the ovens all but gone and the fresh air wafting through while reading a romance set in some faraway place.

"All alone here?" The stranger's voice made her yelp. "Oh, I'm sorry. Did I scare you?"

"We're closed. Come back tomorrow." Amelia stared at the man and instantly recognized his greasy profile. It was Luann's Todd. He took one step up to completely block the back doorway.

"Did I just hear your friend say that your little business here was operating in the black? That's good, right? In the black means you're making good money."

"You need to leave, sir."

"Oh, I'll go. I just wanted to make a suggestion." His face was sickly slick as though he had a fever or something. "My good friend told me that you screwed her when she hired you. She wants a total refund as well as damages. It'll all be in the paperwork her lawyer will deliver. I'm just here as a courtesy. She's willing to drop everything for five thousand dollars."

Amelia didn't speak.

"I'll give you a couple days to think about it. But I'd hate it if anything happened to your business and you couldn't make any more of these cupcakes. I hear people really like them."

Amelia's fists clenched. Aside from her children, whom she'd walk through fire for, the most important thing in Amelia's life was her truck. It was hers. She spent more time in it than in her own home.

"You tell Luann Jameson the next time she wants to threaten me, she can come try and do it herself."

"Luann who?" Todd smirked. Slowly, he backed off the truck. "You just remember what I said. I'll be back." He waved his fingers and disappeared.

Amelia let out her breath and put a hand to her stomach. She wasn't sure if she wanted to scream or puke. Instead, she splashed some cold water on her face and slammed the back door shut, locking it from the inside. She sat at the service window, waiting for Dan.

"Could you identify him if you saw him again?" Dan asked with clenched teeth, smoothing Amelia's hair away from her face.

"Yes. And I think I might know where he is. Lila said that Rusty knows the guy and doesn't like him."

"Of course. If he's a real biker, he's probably at the Twisted Spoke." Dan scratched his chin then pulled Amelia to him and hugged her tightly. "Sometimes I really don't like the fact you are out here by yourself."

"I understand, Dan." She nuzzled into his chest. "But it's my job. Just like it's your job to catch the bad guys. Keep us little guys safe."

"Hmm. I didn't do such a good job of it tonight."

"Look, I know a shakedown when I see it. Whether Luann put him up to this or not, he's a guy looking to make a few quick bucks, thinking he can scare a woman more than he could Gavin over at the Philly Cheese Steak truck or Matthew at the Burrito Wagon."

"Especially Matthew at the Burrito Wagon!" Dan exclaimed, as Matthew was built like those old-fashioned refrigerators from the 1950s.

"So." Amelia slipped her arms around Dan and

squeezed. "Let's go take a chance he's at the Twisted Spoke. Luann thinks her guard dog is scary. Wait until she gets a load of mine."

Dan looked down at her and winked.

"You said it, kid."

He took Amelia by the hand to his car, and within minutes after locking up The Pink Cupcake, they were pulling up in front of the Twisted Spoke restaurant and bar.

The place was busy. Rusty, still being on his sabbatical, had left a huge guy by the name of Roy in charge. Where Rusty was pleasant and enjoyed chatting with regulars and flirting with the girls, Roy was all business. Quick to get the food and drinks served, he didn't mind if someone wanted to kill a few hours at the bar, but they better be buying.

The same went for the fellows who hogged the pool tables. They would play until closing time as long as the waitress was bringing up an order every half hour or so.

"Otherwise, go find a Starbucks to sit in!" Roy often barked. There were still a couple of fights that would break out late on Friday and Saturday nights. But Roy had no problem using Rusty's peacekeeper under the bar. A Louisville Slugger had an almost instant calming effect on those around.

The parking lot was full of cars, pickup trucks, and a couple dozen motorcycles. Bob Segar's "Old Time Rock and Roll" played on the jukebox.

The smell of pulled pork, flame-broiled burgers, and beer filled Amelia's nostrils as they approached the entrance.

"Wait." Dan took Amelia's hand. "Let's scope the place out first. Do you see his bike anywhere?"

"There." She pointed to the exact same bike she had seen at the Four Seasons. Its one distinguishing detail shone in the light of the streetlamp.

"I hate this guy already," Dan muttered. "Would you do me a favor and wait in the car?"

"What? You want to go in there and get him without me? But I want to see his face when you tell him you want to talk to him." She rubbed her stomach.

Dan sighed and scratched his head.

"Okay. Follow me." Instead of going in the front door, Dan walked to the alley where the music wasn't so loud and the back door to the kitchen was wide open to let cool air in.

Politely, Dan knocked on the back door before stepping in. A beefy man in a black T-shirt with no sleeves, and an apron covered in beef and pork blood and sauces turned as he scowled. He held a spatula in his hand while a couple of burgers sizzled on the grill.

"Dan Walishovski," the man croaked. "What are you doing sneaking around here?" He wiped his hands on a towel that was draped over his shoulder and flashed a yellow, crooked smile.

"Hey, Pete." Dan smiled and shook the man's hand before he introduced Amelia.

"I know you. You're that pretty thing that makes the cupcakes with Rusty's gal."

"That's right." Amelia beamed, almost forgetting what she and Dan were there to do.

"Pete, I've got a problem with one of the patrons. You think you can get Roy to help me out?"

"Absolutely. I'm on parole. I don't need no trouble. My granddaughter is turning eight next week. Pop-Pop is going to be at that birthday party." He winked at Amelia, who grinned.

Pete hit a bell, and within a few seconds, Roy was at the door. As soon as he saw Dan, he pushed the swinging kitchen door in and walked up to the detective.

"What can I do for you, Dan?" Roy grumbled. Amelia had to look up over a foot to see in his face. It was a scary sight.

Dan explained that they didn't want to cause any disturbance but needed to speak to Todd.

"Please. Get that trash out my restaurant. Rusty told him more than once he wasn't welcome, but word gets out when the cat's away."

"I'd be grateful, Roy. Thanks."

"What is your granddaughter's name?" Amelia asked quietly as Roy went to summon Todd.

"Crystal." He tapped the photograph taped to the wall above the sink to his right. A black-haired girl with new front teeth grinned back.

"She's beautiful," Amelia whispered.

"Amelia, why don't you stand outside, just in case," Dan said.

She nodded and stepped just out of view but could still hear everything. Pete went back to his grill, and Dan stood next to a tall silver rack of various breads and buns. In just a few minutes, Todd entered the kitchen.

"Who the hell are you?" he snapped at Dan, wiping his nose on the back of his hand.

Dan flashed his badge and identified himself. Pete stayed focused on the grill as if nothing were going on behind him.

"So, Detective." He spat the words. "You want

to tell me why you pulled me away from my pool game?"

"Did you speak to a woman tonight? Good looking. Owns her own business."

"Maybe," Todd answered smugly. He swayed a little and peered at Dan through squinty red eyes. Obviously, happy hour had started for him already. He smelled as though someone had dumped a pitcher of beer over him.

"Well, that woman said you were trying to extort money from her. Any truth to what she said?"

"I don't know what you're talking about." Todd chuckled.

"Okay. So you weren't with a woman this afternoon?"

"I don't remember." Todd looked as if he was enjoying himself.

"You'd remember this woman. Blond hair. Hourglass figure. Wears those kinds of dresses that wrap around real tight." Dan rocked back on his heels.

Amelia was peeking through the crack in the door and saw Todd's jaw go slack. Sobriety slapped him across the face, and he swallowed hard. He thought Dan was talking about *her*. *Not* Luann.

"No. Don't know anyone like that."

"You sure, because she described you, your bike, your tattoos, everything about you."

Amelia wanted to laugh but bit her tongue. Dan was a genius.

"Yeah. I'm sure. Now, are you done?" Amelia could see Todd's fingers twitching.

"Well, I guess if you don't know anyone like that, maybe this woman has you confused with someone else. That's a shame." Dan cleared his throat. "Thank you for your time."

Todd eyed Dan but didn't say a word as he pushed the swinging door in and stomped out of the kitchen. Dan clapped Pete on the back before exiting through the back door and into the alley where Amelia was waiting.

"That was awesome!" she whispered excitedly. "Now what?"

"Listen." Dan pointed his right index finger in the air and looked up to the darkening sky. The sound of a motorcycle rumbling to life cut through the rock music. The tires kicking up stones and peeling across the parking lot and onto the street indicated someone on a motorcycle was leaving in a huge hurry.

"Do you think your friend Bud would mind some visitors?" Dan tilted his head to the right.

"I don't know. But I think once he knew what it was about, he'd be glad to see us. Especially if we came bearing gifts."

Dan looked at Amelia oddly.

"You can't have a proper stakeout without sustenance. You taught me that on the first stakeout you invited me on."

"I knew there was a reason I kept you around."

Dan went back into the Twisted Spoke and picked up three cheeseburgers and a couple of Cokes for the road. Within fifteen minutes, they were pulling down Brightway with the lights off on the car and the police scanner turned down to a quiet murmur.

Amelia showed Dan where Bud had asked her to park. At night, it was almost completely concealed in shadows. Quietly, they exited the vehicle and approached the front door.

"Do you think he's home?" Dan asked.

"Yes. I don't think he goes out too much." Amelia clicked her tongue. "But he did say he has a girlfriend. I hope we won't be interrupting."

Dan laughed outright. Amelia looked at him and shook her head.

"Sorry."

They walked up to the front door and were

nearly blinded with motion sensor porch lights. Amelia pressed the doorbell and then knocked on the door. There was no answer.

"Something doesn't feel right," she said, setting the bags of carryout on the stoop, then she started to walk around to the back of the house. "I'm going around back."

"Wait. We'll both go."

The terrain around the side of Bud's house was rocky and uneven. Amelia was sure he designed it this way on purpose. Why make it easy for the men in black, right? She carefully stepped over smooth, slippery stones then tripped over vine-covered dirt before traipsing over an obstacle course of cut wood and large stones.

"Jeez, one false step, and a person could crack their head open. Or fall into those bushes." She pointed to the right, where a long row of thick shrubs ran along the parameter.

"Be careful. Those are sticker bushes," Dan stated flatly.

"How do you know?"

"Because they just scraped up my entire right side from my neck to my hand."

The lights from Bud's kitchen spilled out onto the yard. Not because they were so bright but because the back door had been kicked outward and was hanging dangerously by one hinge.

"This doesn't make any sense." Dan put his arm in front of Amelia. "Stay behind me. That door was kicked from the inside. Why would Bud do that to his own house?"

"He didn't." Amelia remembered their conversation over tea. "He told me that he had the kitchen rigged like jewelry stores. If someone breaks in, they get trapped in there. Looks like whoever got trapped didn't like Bud's home protection system."

Slowly, they proceeded toward the open door. Once at the top of the porch, Amelia saw Bud lying on the ground. There was blood coming from his head.

"Oh no! Bud!"

The kitchen looked as though a tornado had hit it. The heavy picnic table was pushed to the side, with its benches wedged underneath it. Bud's bureau had been knocked over, and everything in the china cabinet was shattered into a million shards all over the floor. Even his elegant box of teas didn't escape the rampage that took place. They were scattered everywhere. But what broke Amelia's heart was that Bud's Mr. Spock mug was broken beyond repair.

Before he could stop her, Amelia had dashed into the kitchen and carefully felt Bud's wrist.

"He's still warm." She sighed. Dan pulled his cell from his pocket and got 9-1-1 in motion sending an ambulance immediately to Bud's place. Within sixty seconds, the sirens could be heard in the distance.

"Bud? Bud? Can you hear me?" Amelia asked carefully. "It's Amelia Harley."

Bud's eyes fluttered open, and he attempted to move.

"No. Don't move. Your head is bleeding."

"Those bastards," Bud muttered.

"Was it the men in black?" Amelia asked nervously. What if Bud had been right all along and now she was on their radar because of her connection to Bud? What would happen to her or the kids? What about her business?

"No. It was Luann's attack dog."

"Oh, that's better." Amelia sighed.

"What?" Bud snapped.

"Sorry. Just lie still. An ambulance is on the way." Amelia looked up at Dan.

"Bud, can you tell me what happened?"

"Yeah, I'll tell you." Bud winced while trying to talk. "I was served with papers saying that Luann was suing me for property damage because she claimed a tree fell on some shed she had just put up. The tree is on my land, and the shed is on hers." He swallowed hard, prompting Amelia to get him a glass of water. She gently helped him take a sip before he continued.

"Well, I went to investigate said tree. The next thing I know, some guy in a black ski mask is chasing me."

"How do you know it wasn't someone who was, you know, trying to prevent you from finding out 'the truth.'" Amelia air-quoted the last two words.

"Because I could smell the liquor on him." Bud clenched his teeth.

Amelia looked at Dan, who nodded.

The ambulance was down the street. Dan ran out to the edge of the driveway to flag them down, leaving Amelia alone with Bud. She took his hand in hers.

"Help is here. So just relax, and they'll take care of you."

"Can you do me a favor?"

"Of course, Bud."

"Please call Fiona. Tell her what happened, and tell her I'll need her to implement Plan Nine."

"Plan Nine?"

"She'll know." Bud cringed. "That light is killing my eyes." He squinted into the overhead kitchen light and tried to turn his head, but that hurt even more.

"You probably have a concussion," Amelia told him. "So do what the doctors say. Would you like me to see if Dan can get an officer placed outside your hospital room?"

"No. Everything that needs to be done, Fiona will handle it." The corner of Bud's mouth went up slightly in what was sort of a smile. "Thanks, though. I-I appreciate it."

Just then, the paramedics came rushing through the door into the kitchen then pushed Amelia outside while they loaded Bud on a stretcher.

A uniformed police officer began a conversation with Dan, and Amelia could hear Dan instructing him to get the plywood up over the door immediately. Whether Bud's information that he had on secret government agencies and alien sightings was real or not, he didn't deserve to have his home vandalized further.

"Well, what an interesting turn of events." Dan walked back to the front of the house, where he grabbed the bags of food and handed one to

Amelia as he kept one for himself and took a seat on the stoop.

"Poor Bud," Amelia said. "He asked me to call his girlfriend. I better do that now."

"Are you serious?"

"Let me use your phone." She pouted.

"Let me guess. She's long distance in Canada."

"That's what I said, and he nearly bit my head off. No. Her name is Fiona, and she works at the Gary veterinary office." The recorded operator voice asked for city and state before Amelia finally got the digits for the vet's office. A woman who was not Fiona answered the phone but promised to give her the message, including the implementation of Plan Nine.

"Plan Nine?" Dan muttered with a mouth full of burger.

Amelia shrugged as she took a seat next to him and began to eat her own meal.

"I think we should wait until his house is secured. The boys with the plywood company are usually pretty quick. They'll secure that back door, and Bud's place will be safe until he gets back. He must have put up a real fight. I would have never guessed he had it in him."

"What do you think about what he said?"

Amelia covered her mouth as she spoke with it full of food. "About the guy in the ski mask smelling of booze. I was downwind of Todd at the Twisted Spoke, and I'll tell you what—it was Miller Time."

"Yeah. But it doesn't prove anything. You know how many guys are already drunk in this town at this very moment? Too many."

Amelia nodded then snapped her fingers.

"What about his surveillance cameras? He's got this place wired."

"It's a possibility. We'll have to wait until he's released from the hospital. In the meantime, I think I'm going to do a little digging on Todd Coz, and while I'm at it, I think a closer look at Luann Jameson might be in order."

"What are you thinking?"

"Well, it seems to me that a lot of people who are in the vicinity of Luann seem to be having a string of misfortunes. First her son-in-law, then you with the cupcake order, and now Bud. Coincidence?"

"There are no coincidences," Amelia said, wiping her mouth with a napkin.

CHAPTER TWELVE

AMELIA FINALLY GOT home with a sack of McDonald's for the kids. Without mentioning Todd Coz's visit to The Pink Cupcake, she apologized to Adam and Meg for being late.

"That's okay, Mom. I got all my homework done," Meg boasted.

"What about you, Adam?"

"I'll get it done," he muttered nonchalantly.

"Okay, well, when you do get it all done, can you post something online for me?" Amelia yawned as she pulled out the description she and Lila had finalized.

"We need to hire an extra person. Lila and I are overwhelmed, and as much as I'd love to pull you kids out of school and chain you to the truck to work with me every day, making twenty-five cents an hour, there are these silly laws that prevent that." Amelia twisted her lips as she looked at her kids.

"Sure, Mom. What job sites do you want them on?"

"How many are there?"

"Dozens," Adam replied as his mom handed him the piece of paper.

"I'm going to leave that up to you since you seem to know more about it than I do. Is that okay?"

"Sure. Consider it done."

"Thanks, honey. I appreciate it. So what did you guys do while I was gone besides homework and anything but homework?" Amelia pulled out a chair at the kitchen table and flopped down in it.

"Dad called," Adam answered.

"Oh yeah? What did he want?" Amelia felt a tingle of satisfaction as she recalled being thrown out of the Four Seasons and really hoped the word would get back to him.

"He said they were having a nice time and that they'd be home in a few more days and that they had souvenirs for us."

"Well, that sounds nice." Amelia rubbed the back of her neck.

"He also wanted to know what Meg and I thought about moving in with him."

Amelia's heart stopped beating in her chest.

"What?" She was suddenly no longer sleepy.

"He wanted to know if we would consider moving in with him and Jennifer. Something about making it easier on everyone and you wouldn't have to struggle so much."

Amelia knew this had to do with alimony. If he had custody of the kids, he could pay less to her. But that wasn't even the issue. If he took the kids, Amelia would die. They'd become such a good team together. John couldn't possibly be serious about uprooting them.

"What did you tell him?" Amelia was surprised the words came out as calmly as they did.

"We said we'd think about it," Meg said, shoveling half a dozen fries in her mouth at once.

"Okay. Well, guys. I'm beat. I'm going to take a hot shower then probably go to bed." She pushed herself up from the kitchen table. Her legs felt wobbly underneath her.

"Okay, Mom," they both replied.

Amelia literally had to pull herself up the stairs.

She felt dizzy, and the urge to vomit swept over her as she made it to the upstairs landing.

Carefully, with one hand supporting her against the wall and the other waving to help her keep her balance, she made it to her room, closed the door, and dashed into the bathroom.

The burger Dan had bought her came back up and burned her throat. Her eyes watered, and once everything was up and her gut was empty, she felt her heart break.

Quickly, she turned the water on in the shower and sat on the cool tile floor.

The running water was enough to drown out the sobs of rage and frustration that swept over her.

Why would he suddenly want the kids? He couldn't get away from them fast enough when he handed Amelia divorce papers. He had no problem just forgetting about them when everyone in town knew he was sleeping around.

The thought of not seeing the kids every day was too much. Amelia pulled off her clothes and climbed into the tub and let the hot water fall over her. She held her knees tightly and cried into them as she prayed.

Please, God, don't let him take my kids. I'll do anything. Just don't let him take them away from me.

It was true that Amelia was tired. As soon as she crawled into bed, she fell asleep instantly. But she kept waking up every couple of hours with her mind racing. Songs in her head were running in an endless loop. Every time she started to doze, John's proposition to the kids yanked her back to consciousness. Plus, if Luann could do what she did to Bud, what was to stop her from doing something to ruin The Pink Cupcake? It was all too much.

When she finally fell asleep, it was two in the morning, and she had to be up at five.

When the alarm went off, Amelia rubbed her eyes, which were puffy from crying, swallowed hard, and grimaced. Her throat was sore, and she felt achy all over.

"Not now," she whined, her eyes beginning to water. "I've got too much to do."

But when she flung the covers back, an instant chill wrapped around her, causing her arms and legs to pull back beneath the covers like a crab retreating back into its shell.

She waited a couple minutes. Sometimes it just took a few minutes. Slow and steady won the race, so Amelia slowly emerged from the blankets and dropped her feet over the side of the bed.

Once out in the hallway, she went to Meg's room and opened the door. Her daughter was still asleep. Her brown hair was like a halo around her head, and her mouth hung open so she could breathe in a steady rhythm. It reminded Amelia of all the times she checked on her as a baby, listening for that steady breath those first couple of months, so terrified that she might not hear it. But every night she did. Every night for the past fifteen years, Amelia heard her daughter's breathing. She couldn't live without it.

She tiptoed out of the room and shuffled downstairs. While filling her kettle and putting it on the stove, Amelia remembered everything that had happened the night before. But the cotton in her head and the scratch in her throat prevented her from doing anything more than sighing.

She sat down at the kitchen table and listened to the quiet of the house. Normally, this was a pleasant sound. The calm before the stampede that was her kids pounding on the stairs up from the basement and down from the bedroom with requests and complaints and jabs at one another.

It made Amelia's eyes sting again, but she knew it was this oncoming cold that was making her weepy. She let the tears fall, sniffled pitifully, then wiped her eyes and nose with the sleeve of her pajamas.

"Okay, Amelia. Time to pull it together." She stood and held her hands over the heat of the burner as the water began to bubble. Just as she poured herself a cup and dropped in a pouch of chamomile, the phone rang.

Who in the world is calling at this hour? She picked up the ancient landline phone.

"Hello?" she barked.

"Amelia." Dan's voice sounded like a brick hitting the sidewalk. "I'm sorry to call you so early, honey. I need you to come to Food Truck Alley."

Her sore throat and achy body suddenly disappeared.

"What is it?"

"I got a call from your friend Gavin. He was getting his truck ready when he saw it."

"Saw what, Dan?"

"Honey, I'm sorry, but your truck's been vandalized."

Amelia hung up the phone and woke up the kids. She relayed the little bit of information she knew to them quickly, with a calm face and a shrug, as if it were no big deal.

"These things sometimes happen." Amelia

smoothed Meg's hair and patted Adam on the shoulder. "Probably just kids. Punks on a dare or something."

"But Mom, it's your truck." Meg struggled to keep the tears back.

"Hey. I'm sure it's nothing a little spit and polish can't fix. Now you guys take care of yourselves and make sure you get to the bus on time. There are banana muffins in the freezer, or you can always have some fruit. Promise you'll get to school on time?"

"Yes, Mommy," Meg mumbled.

"I'll make sure, Mom," Adam added, gently tugging his sister's hair to make her smile.

"Okay. If there is any big deal, I'll call the school. So if you don't hear from me, you'll know it's no big deal."

Amelia clenched her teeth as she went into her room and quickly dressed. Without any makeup or even a shower, she dashed out of the house and sped in her sedan to Food Truck Alley.

When she got there, she saw the red and blue lights of one squad car and Dan's unmarked police car. She looked at her truck and wasn't sure what to think.

First of all, the tires were still intact. Had those

been slashed, it would have run her about a thousand dollars to replace them. Someone had dumped a couple cans of garbage around the truck, so it smelled terrible and the flies were pretty gross. But still, picking up the garbage was annoying and unsanitary but not the worst thing in the world.

It was the scratches in the paint that made Amelia mad. The obscene names they scratched in the paint were not just rude, but so childish.

"I think we'll be able to sand this off and paint over it," Dan said soothingly. "But before we do, we have to photograph them and maybe dust for some fingerprints. I'm sorry, but it will have to stay like this for today. Maybe tomorrow, too."

"Losing two days of work will set me back. I won't make my monthly quota."

"I'm sorry, Amelia."

"It isn't your fault." She slumped. "You know what? This isn't as bad as I thought it was going to be. I expected the engine to be ripped out and my tires slashed, and well, this looks like something…a girl would do."

"What do you mean?"

"I mean I think Luann Jameson would have done this. Todd Coz would have slashed my tires and torn up my engine. But it wasn't him."

"Detective?" The uniformed police officer on the scene called to Dan. "We've got a witness who says they saw a woman running from the scene early this morning." Gavin waved to Amelia. He was the witness.

Amelia looked up at Dan, smiled, sniffled, and wiped her nose with the back of her hand.

"Sorry. I'm getting a cold."

CHAPTER THIRTEEN

"TODD COZ ISN'T the brightest bulb on the tree," Dan said to Amelia as he drove her to the police station. She'd need to fill out a report. "I'm betting that with the right incentive, he can be very reasonable and accommodating."

"What have you got in mind?" Amelia said, pulling a paper napkin from the glove compartment and using it to blow her nose.

"Officer Vincent is on his way right now to pick him up and bring him to the station for questioning. I think you're right about the vandalism, and with Gavin's statement, we've got a vague blueprint. But it's Todd who will give us all the correct measurements to make sure everything fits."

"How can you be sure he plays ball?"

"Guys like him don't mind bragging about the stuff they did do, but they don't like being accused of something they didn't do. Especially something as pitiful as scribbling a couple of swear words on a food truck."

"So you're going to manipulate his ego?"

"Am I ever." Dan's face remained stoic, and Amelia saw him squeeze the steering wheel. He was as mad as she was, as if they'd done something to his property, too.

"Ugh," she griped then swallowed. "I didn't get a chance to swallow a gulp of Nyquil or even grab some cough drops. Sore throats are the worst." She rubbed the front of her neck.

"We might have something at the station." Dan patted her leg.

When they finally reached the station, Officer Vincent was already there.

"He's in Room C," he told Dan. "And mad he was woken up so early."

"Got it." Dan looked at Amelia. "Come on."

The police station was quieter at this hour of the morning. Fresh coffee had been put on and made the place smell good. The police on duty chitchatted or were busy at their desks, working on that endless amount of paperwork all police had to muddle through. Now was the time to get to it before the city woke up and started picking at itself.

Dan led Amelia down the hallway to an observation room.

"I'm sure you've seen these on television. He can't see you or hear you. But you can see and hear him. We'll get your paperwork started after I talk to him."

Amelia nodded and took a seat on a metal folding chair in front of the two-way mirror. Almost directly across from her was Todd Coz. His skin was glistening like the other times she'd seen him. His hair was a mess, and he was wearing jeans and a different Harley-Davidson T-shirt that was inside out. Obviously, he'd dressed in a hurry.

"Good morning, Mr. Coz." Dan's voice was heavy. "I'm sorry to have gotten you out of bed so early. Yikes. You pounding meat with your fists? Rocky Balboa workout routine?"

"Yeah. What is this all about? You in love with me or something? Is that why you are harassing me? Showing up where I drink. Having me brought here? Look, I can hardly blame you, but I'm not into dudes."

"A food truck was vandalized last night. The

woman who owns it claims you paid her a visit yesterday. Tried to get some money out of her."

"I don't know anything about it."

"Normally, that would be a good enough answer, but it seems we've got a witness who also says she saw you at the food truck."

Todd tilted his head and blinked lazily at Dan.

"The call came in this morning. Now, I hate to tell you this, but the woman who said she'd identify you in a lineup, well, she's a pillar in the community. People know her. They trust her. She's got no dog in the fight. She'd never associate with the likes of you."

"I don't believe you. You're lying."

Amelia saw Todd swallow hard, as he had the night before when Dan described Luann to him.

"Just do me a favor, Todd. Look in that mirror." Dan pointed to the exact spot Amelia was sitting in.

"I didn't vandalize any truck!" Todd yelled. "I only went to scare the lady that worked there because..." Todd stopped talking. It was obvious he wanted to say something, but there was some force holding his tongue.

"Well, you don't have to tell me anything, Todd. You can request a lawyer at any time. But this woman who says she saw you vandalize the food truck said you were also stalking her daughter. That she can't prove it but thinks you had something to do with the death of Greg Scottson. Is there any truth to that?"

"Luann! You lying bi—"

"Shut up!" Dan yelled. "Todd Coz, you have the right to remain silent." Dan stood, pulled his handcuffs from the back of his belt, and secured them around Todd's wrists. He finished reading Todd his rights and asked him if he wanted to end the interview.

Amelia watched as the gears slowly shifted and whirred in his head as he thought of what to do.

"No. I'll talk. I've got a lot to say." He glared at the mirror, thinking Luann was sitting where Amelia was, not knowing he had been played by one of the oldest shell games ever.

Dan told Todd to sit tight and he'd bring him some coffee or a cola if he wanted one. Of course, Todd said he'd like both. After leaving the room, Dan opened the door for Amelia.

"That was flipping awesome," she whispered before coughing in her hand. "Now what are you going to do?"

"I'm going to get him his coffee and Coke and see what he has to say."

"Can I listen? This is better than television." Amelia sniffled.

"Yeah. You want a coffee, too?"

Amelia nodded and took her seat again. She studied Todd as he sat there. He didn't look the least bit nervous. Why? What did he have up his sleeve that made him so calm?

Officer Vincent brought Amelia her coffee and stayed to observe Dan's questioning. Dan entered the interrogation room and placed a hot coffee and cold Coke in front of Todd before taking a seat.

"Why don't you just start from the beginning?" Dan suggested. His voice had become quieter.

"I tell you what, Detective. I knew that woman was trouble the first time I laid eyes on her." He chuckled bitterly. Todd explained how he and Luann had met. She had shown up at the Twisted Spoke wearing tight blue jeans and some T-shirt that had something on it. He couldn't remember since it wasn't what was on the shirt but inside it that he was interested in.

"We had a couple drinks then ended up in the backseat of her Lexus. Those really are nice cars." He winked at Dan with a smirk.

Todd went on to explain that he and Luann had developed a kind of relationship.

"You know, a friends with benefits kind of thing."

"Why do you think a woman like Luann would want a guy like you?" Dan sipped his own coffee. "I'm not trying to be rude, but let's not BS each other."

"No, I hear what you're saying. Look, she had an itch. Wanted to walk on the wild side. You'd be surprised how many women like the bad boys. Hell, I bet your daughter would be on the back of my bike with just a few pretty words and a smile."

Dan didn't move, but Amelia shifted in her seat. If she could, she would have slapped him for that comment. Something his mother should have done years ago.

"Well, things are going just fine for several months. Then she starts telling me she needs money, right? She's driving a Lexus. She lives in Sarkis Estates. She gets her nails done once a week and professional bikini waxing and all those kinds of things. From where I'm sitting, she don't need anything."

"So what did you tell her?" Dan asked.

"I said with a body like hers, she shouldn't have any problem making money." Todd cackled as though he had recited the funniest joke ever.

"I'll bet she didn't like that," Dan said to urge him to keep going.

"She acted like she didn't, but I know Luann. It stroked her ego." Todd pulled the pop-top on his can of Coke and took a sip. "So now she was saying she had to get her daughter married off. That would help solve her money problems, she said."

"Had you ever met her daughter?"

"Never once. So the idea that I was stalking *her* is an outright lie. I never met the girl in my life."

"Had Luann mentioned her daughter dating Greg Scottson to you?"

"Not until after the marriage. I had no idea. Like I said, Luann and I weren't exactly picking out china patterns together. We had a physical relationship, and that was it. She usually left family stuff outside the motel room, if you catch my meaning."

"Yeah, I got it." Dan sighed.

"So she tells me that Greg is no good for her daughter. That he's married her for her money and that he beats her."

"Really."

"Yup. She told me that the guy made her take all her clothes off and beat her with a belt everywhere her clothes would be. So when she went out no one would see the bruises."

"And you believed Luann?"

"I knew Greg by reputation only. I never heard anyone say he was a woman beater, but I also never asked. If that is what he was up to, then I think he deserved to slip and fall off that roof."

"Did you push him? As a favor for Luann?"

Todd looked to the left. It was as if he realized he hadn't really helped himself, telling Dan any of this.

"No," Todd snapped. "No. I did not. But-But Luann did talk about having him removed from the scene. She did ask me if I knew anyone who could make an accident happen."

Amelia could tell Todd was lying. He scooted in his chair and slicked back his hair and stared at Dan as if direct eye contact would convince Dan he was telling the truth.

"What did you tell her?"

"I said I might."

"Then what?"

"Well, I gave her the name of a guy and then left it at that."

"What was the name?" Dan took out his pen and paper and looked at Todd.

"Um, Mike. That's all I know."

"You don't know his last name?"

"No."

"So you expect me to believe that you just mention to Luann some guy named Mike, and she hired him to kill her son-in-law based on that little bit of information?"

"Look, I don't know what she did with the information I gave her!" Todd shouted. "But I didn't push anyone off a roof!"

"What about Bud Fetzer? He was beat up pretty bad last night. You know anything about that?"

"Okay, yeah, I did that. Luann said that little freak was spying on her and her daughter. Some kind of fatal-attraction thing. Have you seen the cameras he's got all over his house? So I taught him a lesson."

"Actually, I have seen the cameras all over Mr. Fetzer's house. I've also seen the telescope he has that faces the Jameson house. It's almost directly aligned with their roof. Funny, isn't it?"

"What?" Todd scratched his chin and looked at Dan as if he'd just asked him to solve a calculus problem in his head.

"Yeah, Bud's got cameras and a telescope and a couple of other devices taking in the sights all around his property. In fact, it's funny because when I talked to Bud, he told me that he saw a man who fits your description on the roof when Greg fell. That's funny, isn't it?"

That was it for Todd.

"I think I'll wait for my lawyer."

"I hate to say it, but I think that is very wise, Todd. But thanks for communicating with me. You want another coffee? Coke?"

Todd sat with his cuffed hands in his lap and scowled at Dan. When he came out of the room, Amelia was giddy.

"What do you do now?" She was going to ask for details, but a loud, familiar voice was heard in the bull pen, drawing Dan's attention. Amelia followed behind.

"I really don't know what this could be about. I don't understand why no one will tell me anything." Luann Jameson pouted.

"Just have a seat, Ms. Jameson," Officer Vincent ordered. "Detective Walishovski will be right with you."

"Well, I hope so. I've got a property showing at eight o'clock. If I lose this sale because of this, I'll be very upset."

"Don't worry, Mrs. Jameson." Dan strolled out to the bull pen. "Would you mind coming with me?" He waved her on.

Every eye was on Luann as she slinked through the desks, sashaying like a Miss Universe contestant on a stage. She was wearing black skinny jeans and heels with a tight navy-blue T-shirt that dipped down daringly in the front. But the minute she saw Amelia, her feet tangled up for a second before she regained her composure.

She looked past Amelia as if she didn't see her at all.

While Dan held the door to Interrogation Room B open for her, he waved to Amelia. Without a word, she slipped into the observation room and sat down as she had when she watched Todd.

"What is this all about, Detective?" She batted her eyes at Dan and pushed her cleavage up as she folded her hands in her lap.

"We've got a problem regarding the investigation into your son-in-law's death."

"Investigation? He fell off the roof. He was stoned and probably drunk."

"Well, that's odd that you say that, because the autopsy revealed there were no amounts of marijuana or alcohol or any other narcotic in his system. How do you think that can be?"

"The test was probably done wrong." She shook her head, letting her blond hair bounce around her face. "You know how hard it is to get good help these days."

"Yeah, help like Todd Coz helped you kill your son-in-law."

"Who?" she asked calmly.

"Todd Coz. Biker. Bit of a bad boy."

Luann laughed.

"Do I look like the type of woman who dates bikers? I'm sure you've heard of my late husband. My standards are very high, Detective." She looked down at her long, manicured fingernails then back up at Dan.

"But your daughter fell in love with a mechanic. Were you disappointed?"

"I wanted my daughter to be happy. But I sheltered her so much. She gave her heart to the first guy who had the nerve to come up to her. What could I do? I can't stand in the way of my daughter's happiness."

Amelia remembered the insurance policy on Colleen's nightstand. Colleen was due to receive six million dollars in the event Greg died. The papers hadn't been signed yet. When Amelia was hiding under the bed, she heard Luann trying to get Colleen to sign the papers fast.

She jumped up and left the room to knock on the door, interrupting Dan's interrogation.

"What is it?" Dan asked quietly, shutting the door behind him while Luann waited. Amelia told him about the policy.

"With everything else that went on that day, I totally forgot about it until now. Todd said Luann kept saying she needed money. Do you think this could be an elaborate insurance scam?"

Dan walked to the bull pen and asked Officer Vincent to run a skip-trace on Luann Jameson. Her address was in the file on his desk. Dan went back to the interrogation room, leaving Amelia in the bull pen.

When he returned, it had been just a minute, and Officer Vincent was back with a long printout of paper.

Dan grinned.

"This is interesting."

"What is it?" Amelia wiped sweat from her head. She was starting to feel very warm.

"It looks like Luann Jameson is in debt almost three quarters of a million dollars. Greg Scottson was her meal ticket. A poor kid who was just a mechanic and who happened to like her daughter. He was expendable."

Amelia felt weak and sat down.

Before Dan could get back to Luann in Interrogation Room B, a pretty young girl who looked like a more conservative, modest version of Luann came into the station. She had a file with her and appeared to have been crying.

"Colleen?" Amelia waved nervously. Was she really seeing her, or had she come down with a fever and was hallucinating?

Colleen smiled and came up to Amelia.

"Hi, Mrs. Harley. Funny meeting you here. I hope everything is all right," she said politely.

"Just some vandals hit my food truck. I'm just filing a report."

The smile fell from Colleen's face.

"So she did do it."

Amelia looked up to Dan, who had taken a step closer.

"Colleen, this is Detective Dan Walishovski."

"Hello, Detective. I'm Colleen Scottson. I'm hoping someone can help me."

"I'll do my best, miss."

"My mother killed my husband. I'd like to press charges."

Amelia and Dan could have been knocked over by a feather.

"Excuse me, Miss Scottson. Why don't you come with me where we can talk in private?"

"I don't need to talk in private, Detective." Colleen squared her shoulders. "Everyone here knows who my mother is. Only I know *what* she is. And I want to make sure that justice is done."

"Have a seat, Miss Scottson."

"I'm fine to stand," she protested. "It's all right here. My mother had spent my stepfather's entire fortune. She'd even tapped into my account, leaving me with barely anything left in my trust." She handed over to Dan a thick manila folder. "It's all right here. Her bank transactions. My signature that she forged. The debtors who have been trying to chase her down. And of course, the insurance policy she took out on Greg."

"You didn't take it out?" Dan asked, looking through all the papers.

"I had no idea it existed. Not until after his 'accident.'" Colleen used air quotes for emphasis. "My mother's fingerprints are all over it. She forged my signature on that, too."

"Colleen, do you know who Todd Coz is?"

"No. I have no idea. But I saw his name on a couple of personal checks. I just assumed he was a masseuse or a tennis instructor or one of the dozens of people she pays to be around her. Why? Who is he?"

"We think he's the man who pushed your husband off the roof."

Colleen's bottom lip began to tremble, and tears fell from her eyes.

"Right. Because my mother would never do the dirty work. She'd pay someone to do it. She'd pay them with a check." Colleen shook her head.

Everyone stood still in the bull pen for a few minutes. Finally, Dan spoke.

"We have your mother in an office. With this information, we are going to have to put her under arrest. Do you want to talk to her before we do that?"

Colleen looked at the floor then up at Dan.

"I don't have anything to say to her, Detective."

Just then, a ruckus could be heard down the hallway.

"If I'm not being charged with anything, I refuse to wait here any longer. This is unwarranted detainment, and I..." Luann froze when she saw Colleen.

Amelia started to shake as the chills from her fever took hold of her. But she watched the mother and daughter with morbid fascination.

"Mrs. Jameson," Dan said. "Your daughter has provided us with some very important information."

Luann still stared at her daughter.

"I'm going to need you to put your hands behind your back. You are under arrest for conspiracy to commit murder of Greg Scottson. You have the right to remain silent."

"Colleen, what have you done?" Luann asked. "What have you told them? You're out of your mind with grief. Tell them! Tell them that you didn't mean it! Colleen!"

"He loved me, Mom, and you had him killed." Colleen faced her mother. "And you trashed Amelia's truck. Just admit it. You said you were going to, and you did it. You are pathetic."

"I didn't do it! I didn't do any of it! Todd Coz did it! Honey, he was stalking you! He was obsessed with you, and when he found out you were married to Greg, he took it out on him. He pushed him off the roof!"

"You're a liar," Colleen replied, almost whisper-ing. "Detective, call me if you need me. My contact information is in the file."

The entire police station fell silent as Colleen walked out. The only sound was the ragged gasps of Luann's breathing. Amelia turned to look at her. This time, Luann really didn't see Amelia. She was staring into space. Her entire body was taut like a bow when an arrow is about to be fired. How long she'd be able to sustain that was anyone's guess. But Amelia didn't want to be around when she snapped and the reality of the situation settled in.

Officer Vincent took Luann by the arm and led her out of the bull pen. Amelia assumed she was being booked and fingerprinted and all that jazz.

"I'm going to take you home, Amelia," Dan said, offering her his hand. "I don't know if you know it, but you are radiating heat off your body."

"Don't get fresh with me, Detective," she muttered.

"You have a fever, don't you," he stated rather than asked.

"I wasn't feeling good this morning. I told you. It's just all caught up with me."

"Let's get you home."

As she climbed into his car, she felt her eyes burning with tears.

"John's talking about having the kids live with him. When they told me he called last night and that he suggested it, I think my body just gave up."

"He's done this before." Dan pinched his

eyebrows together. "He's asked the kids, and they've said no. They'll say no again," Dan said soothingly.

"It's just that he always decides to make these plans when I'm least prepared to deal with them. Why does he do that? Why doesn't he ask me first?"

"When you were married, did he ever ask you first?" Dan's voice was angry. Not at Amelia but at her ex-husband, who he currently wanted to punch in the nose.

"No. He didn't. He never did."

"Then not much has changed on his end. But everything has changed on your end, and I think that is what is really bothering him."

"But he's got everything. The fancy job with the fancy salary and the trophy wife and the huge house. Why would he try to take the kids? He never wanted them before," Amelia whined. "I'm sorry." She blubbered. "It's this bug. I don't feel good, and I wish I had my mama."

Dan smiled and rubbed her cheek gently as he drove to her house.

Once there, he ran her a hot shower, left her flannel pajamas for her to get dressed in, then helped her get into bed before he put on a pot of tea.

"Dan, I can't thank you enough," she said as the

shot of Nyquil she took started to take hold. "I've made you late for work. You can go. I don't need anyone."

"That's not true," he murmured while he held her hand and sat on the side of the bed. "I can't bring back your mama, but I called for reinforcements."

At that second, the front door was unlocked, opened, and slammed shut.

"We're up here!" Dan yelled.

"Lord, I hope you both are decent," Lila called up the steps.

Amelia's eyes teared up, but she smiled.

"Look at this. When Dan called me about the truck, I knew you'd take it hard, but honey, we can get that paint job done in no time. I've already got a couple guys from the Twisted Spoke cleaning up the garbage for us."

"Really?" Amelia yawned.

"I told Rusty over the phone, and he said not to worry. When I went out there to see for myself, they were already almost done. Gavin and the folks from the Burrito Wagon were also pitching in."

"I feel like George Bailey from *It's a Wonderful Life*," Amelia replied with heavy eyes.

"I do hope we find out who did it," Lila hissed.

"We did." Amelia yawned again. "I'll tell you all about it. As soon as I wake up."

"That sounds perfect," Lila replied, pulling the blankets up around her friend. "I'll be reading downstairs. Call me when you wake up."

"Thanks, Lila. Thanks, Dan." She grinned slyly at them. "I knew you guys were keepers."

"Oh yeah? How did you know that?" Lila asked.

Amelia looked lovingly at Dan.

"I went with my gut."

RECIPE 1: VANILLA CHERRY CUPCAKES

Makes 24

Ingredients:

- 2 cups flour + 2 tbsp. for coating cherries
- 3 large eggs
- 1 tsp baking powder
- 1 tsp baking soda
- ¼ tsp sea salt
- ¾ cup organic sugar
- ¼ cup honey
- 1 tsp pure vanilla extract
- ½ cup unsalted butter, melted
- 1 ½ cups Greek yogurt
- 3 cups pitted and chopped fresh cherries

Frosting:

- 8 ounces cream cheese, softened
- ½ cup organic sugar
- 3 cups heavy cream
- 24 fresh cherries to top each cupcake

Preheat oven to 350 F. Line pan with cupcake liners.

In a bowl, combine flour, baking powder, baking soda, and salt. Set aside.

Rinse, cut, pit, and chop cherries. Set aside in a bowl.

In another bowl, beat eggs and sugar on high for about 5 minutes, or until foamy and thick. Add honey and vanilla. Beat for 2 more minutes.

Add melted butter and Greek yogurt. Beat on medium until combined. Sift and mix in flour in two separate additions. Mix carefully not to deflate air bubbles.

Sprinkle cherries with flour. Add cherries in the batter and gently mix.

Fill each liner up 3/4 with batter. Bake for 20 minutes. Let cool before frosting.

Frosting: Beat cream cheese and sugar until smooth and sugar is completely dissolved. Add vanilla extract. Mix just until combined. Add heavy cream. Start on low and gradually increase mixing speed to prevent splatters. Beat cream until thick, around 1-2 minutes.

Transfer into a piping bag to frost cupcakes. Top each cupcake with a cherry. Can refrigerate cupcakes in a closed container.

RECIPE 2: GREEN TEA CUPCAKES

Makes 12. Not *the healthy version!*

Ingredients
- 1 cup cake flour
- 1/2 cup milk
- 1/4 cup butter, softened
- 3/4 cup sugar
- 1 large egg
- 2 tbsp unsweetened matcha
- 1/2 tsp baking powder
- 1/4 tsp baking soda
- 1/4 tsp salt
- 1 tsp almond extract

Frosting:

- 2 cups confectioner's sugar
- 4 tbsp butter, lightly softened
- 8 ounces cream cheese, softened
- 1 tbsp unsweetened matcha

Preheat oven to 350 F. Line pan with 12 cupcake liners.

Sift flour, matcha powder, baking soda, and salt in a bowl.

In another bowl, beat butter and sugar with an electric mixer or beater at medium-high speed for up to 5 minutes or until light and fluffy. Add egg and almond extract and mix well.

Over low speed, add in the dry ingredients. Add milk. Mix until combined.

Pour batter into cupcakes and bake for 16-18 minutes. Let cool in the pan before transferring to wire rack.

Frosting: In a bowl, sift together confectioner's sugar and matcha powder. Mix well.

In another bowl, cream butter and cream cheese over medium speed. Add in dry ingredients and mix until combined.

Add frosting to a piping bag to pipe over cooled cupcakes.

Can refrigerate the cupcakes in a covered container for up to 5 days.

ABOUT THE AUTHOR

Harper Lin is the *USA TODAY* bestselling author of 6 cozy mystery series including *The Patisserie Mysteries* and *The Cape Bay Cafe Mysteries*.

When she's not reading or writing mysteries, she loves going to yoga classes, hiking, and hanging out with her family and friends.

www.HarperLin.com

www.ingramcontent.com/pod-product-compliance
Lightning Source LLC
Chambersburg PA
CBHW050849180626
46814CB00007B/2692